Decaf
Mushrooms

2nd edition, 2021

a mindfully rehashed collection
of stories and other items
by Robert Arnott

The Runner, The Birks, today's condiment flash fiction, La manutention de l'infini, To the Moon, I took my slippers, Carelessness and dream sequence idea #1 feature for the first time in this second edition.

All other material featured in the first edition of *Decaf Mushrooms* (first published by CreateSpace (2016) and subsequently by Daan Creaties (2017)), which combined two ebooks, *The Mushroom Surpriser* (2014) and *Decaf Latte* (2015).

The Longest Night was first published online in *Éclat Fiction*, issue 1, January 2012.

My Belgian Muzhik was first published in *The New Writer* issue 110, spring 2012, having been commended in the 2010 prose & poetry prize competition.

Leaving St Fillans was shortlisted for the Fish Poetry Prize 2013.

A slightly longer version of 'Brodsky' was longlisted for the Lightship short story competition in 2011.

Through the Sky was longlisted for the Fish Short Story Prize 2013-14, and appeared in the first edition of *Decaf Mushrooms* under the title 'Man Surrounded'.

also by Robert Arnott:

novel:
The Overturning

~~fictional football website:~~
~~TransRegional Soccer (www.transregionalsport.net)~~

DECAF MUSHROOMS

THE RUNNER

One

Fuck.

Lost count again.

What was it – 57? Or 59. Or 69, even?

Hopeless.

And the realisation, of course, that he ought to put them in identical piles, because that's the way to do it. Ought to have done that to start off with. Obvious. The pennies in piles of 10, and the 2ps in piles of five, also making 10p a stack.

But what would people think, whoever's watching him in here? Here's some daft laddie who cannae count? This gangly, glaikit youth who's just opened up his piggy bank? (yes) Putting his pennies in the bank, like Daddy says to? (yes)

Along, of course, with the £20 birthday cheque from Uncle Tom and Auntie Rhona, and the £15 birthday cheque from Auntie Edith, because nobody, not even a cantankerous minor, goes to a bank just to deposit £6 in coppers.

And here come the hot red cheeks. Even a bit of shaking in the legs.

That's legs with blue and black trainers and ill-fitting jeans on them, just so you know, and a black t-shirt featuring the word 'Alba' on it, in the middle of an unconvincing, lopsided Celtic-ish design.

Even if the other couple of customers, the two old ladies, hadn't registered his presence, the staff must have been starting to wonder what he was actually doing in here. Must be looking at him. Thinking they might need to click open the door along at the end of the counter and come over to him to ask if he's all right.

He wished (he, Gavin, that's Gavin Jamieson, which is me, who's recounting this) that the world would stop, or that the whole turreted TSB would just subside into the river, or explode, or take off into space, or that something else very dramatic would occur so that he didn't have to humiliate himself by counting his coppers all over again.

It did.

Alexander (sometimes 'Sandy') Bell, inventor of not a single telephone, enters the bank at 10.39 am, approaches the teller, where there is no queue, because Gavin is faffing with his coppers and the two old ladies are still standing in the middle of the floor talking about – I kid you not – cake, and he (Alexander 'Sandy' Bell, who has spent not a second of his life listening to fiddlers in Sandy Bell's famous pub) points the sawn-off shotgun at Moira, Morag or Dawn (why pretend I can remember what her name was?) and says:

Put all the money in the bag!

For the purposes of narrative fidelity that should be a full stop, because he just said it, not raising his voice, not shouting. But that would look a bit weird somehow. Interactions vocalised in the course of hold-ups demand exclamation marks, surely.

The reason he didn't raise his voice was that he didn't especially want people to know what he was doing. That is, people other than Moira/Morag/Dawn, who really had to know what he was doing, because she was the person in the firing... sorry.

No, actually, yes, very much the firing line, for fetching the banknotes that A. Bell very much wanted to obtain.

Hence, also, the classic *sawn-off* characteristic of his gun.

Now, I've since compared notes on hold-ups with various colleagues, and there have been some good ones.

Like,

- Put the money in the bag!
- No, no, no. That's just a butter knife you've got there, son.

And there's the stories I've heard about other people's ID parades and police interviews and so on. Honestly, I should tell you. Very funny. All bundled into the same polis van together. Witness and crook. Chatting and offering each other fags. Can you imagine?

But I'm getting ahead of myself.

Gavin immediately anticipated the statement he'd be giving and the ID parade he would be attending in a few days' time, so he checked his watch and noted A. Bell's voluminous curly hair and his stick-thin legs, to which the attention of Gavin and, possibly, the old ladies, was drawn by dint of the catastrophically tight drainpipe jeans.

He didn't see the boggley eyes of A. Bell until the ID parade, but their boggleyness seemed entirely unsurprising once he did see them, somehow. Thyroid problem?

The reason that A. Bell, and hence also Gavin, Moira/Morag/Dawn, the bank manager and the two old ladies, attended the ID parade was that he (A. Bell) made a fucking awful job of getting away with the bag of money. Discarding his jacket in the river, which was hardly going to be enough to deflect anyone from his cartoonish distinguishing features, he sprinted along the walkway and reached the local park, about half a mile away, and hid among some bushes, where he was discovered, within approximately four minutes, by police dogs and officers.

That's the park just next to the police headquarters.

Just think: can you honestly imagine a *Sandy* executing a successful heist? Thinking not. Ditto *Bob* or *Glen*.

His boggley eyes rolled upwards with irritation – genuine irritation – upon Gavin's unhesitant identification of him, which he made by saying "Yes. Number four."

Gavin and the old ladies spoke briefly to one another, in a sort of reunion of surviving customers, except that their ordeal had involved nothing more than standing behind A. Bell's narrow back for about a minute, taking note of his above-mentioned disastrously memorable features, which led to his swift incarceration, and not at all his hoped-for enjoyment of £3,500 or so, mainly in Clydesdale twenties.

So, the point is this.

And all of that happened, by the way. Like, honest-to-god happened.

The point is this: that the branch manager, D. Stewart, offered Gavin employment that day, the day of the ID parade. Meaning a summer job at the bank, to start off with, leading, let's say for the sake of argument, to a lifelong career in banking. Gavin did not accept the offer, because he was

3

timid and didn't believe that working was a credible thing to do while he was still attending school, and also because his family was not impoverished, and so he had no drive to earn money, even though he now legally had the opportunity to do so outwith termtime. But mainly because he was shy. He did accept the chocolate biscuits and mug of coffee at the police station quite comfortably, but he did not accept that he should start the said career in banking. The thing is that he could have done, and he would eventually have become a branch manager. Let's say.

He didn't, though, so now ('now' meaning in his mid forties), after a rather hard-to-summarise 'career', if you can call it that, Gavin is a secret agent.

*

Now, you're staring at me like I'm not allowed to stop there. Or even pause? You've no questions?

Like this isn't a conversation. Or can't be a conversation.

You have challenged me to tell you my stories, so this is me telling you some stories.

- I haven't "challenged" you. But please go on.

- Okay.

I hope you don't mind me starting with that bank thing, but it was the first thing that really struck me when I started thinking about the… you know: the career trajectory; the life course; the *parcours de vie*, yes?

Mine, though. You're not telling me yours. That's for another time, and it won't be me who hears that.

This'll be a bit of everything, then: Beirut before the explosion; Moscow before Putin; me before I got incredibly fat and half-bald.

You challenged me to do this in the context, obviously, that I am paying you, as a professional.

- Paying me? Only my expenses!

- We don't need to dwell on that.

- And I haven't 'challenged' you. And it's not as if my expenses, which are pretty insubstantial in the scheme of things, are coming out of your pocket. And don't be ridiculous: you're not "incredibly fat."

- All right.

- I do have a question for you, though.

- Yes?

- The bank robber. Bell. You feel contempt for him.

- Um… No, I don't think so.

- You can see how I might have got that impression.

- Yes. No, I understand. I think I see where you're heading.

- Why did this man try to rob your local bank, do you think?

- I see what you're getting at.

- What would you say to him if you ever met him?

- I… I don't know, I suppose. It was just…

- Just a character to you. In your story.

- But… As I said—

- It's all true. I know that. But also true was Bell's terrible, terrible situation, whatever it might have been, his desperation, the intolerable pressure on him, building up to that last resort of going in there with the gun.

- Well. Possibly.

- Not greed, we might assume.

- I take your point.

- You could reflect on it, perhaps. His incarceration, whether it was for the first time or the fifth time: the inevitable cycle; the crushing of opportunity. To you: "Guess what happened when I went to the bank this morning?"

- Okay. Now, before I go any further, you need to know that some of these next things involve secret information.

- Masterful regaining control of the conversation there. Well done.

- You see, I know people who've had secrets, people who've pissed away their secrets and the money that goes with it, and people who I can only suspect of having secrets, because they're actually good at it.

I don't like to think of myself as fat, but maybe I'm a bit fat.

- I'm not going to discuss that. But *can* you keep secrets, Gavin?

- I do keep secrets.

- And are you going to tell me all about that, then?

- Yes.

I know whatever I say will go no further, so to speak. You're a professional, after all.

- My professionalism – indeed, my *profession* – isn't the point here.

- It partly is, though.

- Yes… Yes, you're quite right. But only partly.

- It's what got you into this room.

- Is it?

So anyway… Taking things from the beginning?

- Pretty much. Well. Not quite, actually: I might jump around a bit. You know how it goes.

- Right.

- Okay.

- Okay. And we can get more coffee at any point, I understand.

- Yes. That's right.

This next bit can be Chapter Two, I suppose.

Two

Gavin is sitting on a bar stool inside, or possibly just outside (you'd understand if you could see the place), the Old Albion Pub on the main drag in Mar Mikhael, in east (hence predominantly Christian, hence hosting quite a lot of lively bars) Beirut.

(Sorry about all the brackets, by the way. I'll try and cut down.)

A surprisingly tall man with long hair, presumably Lebanese but who's to know, wearing new blue jeans, something like cowboy boots and a sky-blue t-shirt with the puzzling slogan 'Don't Worry About Your Shit Person' in black lettering, approaches him, and sits down.

- Masa al-khair, Gavin offers.
- Masa al-noor.
- Shukran, Gavin adds, on being handed a padded envelope.
- Take this to Mark Smith in London.
- I will, Gavin responds.

Now, 'Mark Smith' was a secret reference to Zachariah Smyth (who would guess it was really 'Smyth'? – ha ha!) (Sorry. The brackets). And, yes, in London.

This was all a bit quick. In fact, it could have ended immediately, the envelope already being in Gavin's old Karrimor, but to our hero's pleasure, the long-haired man suggests they enjoy a beer seeing as they're there, and so they discuss English football for a bit over a cold Almaza or two, and then the man whizzes off, and then Gavin makes his more unhurried way back towards his apartment.

Now… At that point, I still had one more day in Lebanon.

- Woah!
- What?

7

- You've gone into the first person.

- Oh. Does it matter?

- Emm... Actually, I wonder if it might be easier. Did you do that on purpose?

- Good lord, no. I'm always doing that. And tenses. Sorry.

- Tenses?

- Past tense or dramatic present: I start off with one and then just lapse into the other one, and I don't even notice. Have I been doing that? I don't even know.

Which is annoying, because I think I understand tenses, like, *extremely well*, but I still always do that. Sorry.

- No need to apologise to *me*!

- Okay.

- Look. Just don't worry about it. Do what comes naturally. How you express yourself may potentially prove important, but that's for me to think about, not you.

- Thanks.

Okay, so I had the rest of that evening, with a trip out of town coming up the next day, so I decided to take a stroll. I stopped off at an Armenian restaurant and had some of those tiny little firm things a bit like wee ravioli...

- What?

- *Firm things*. Ravioli. But smaller, and harder. Can't remember what they're called. And half a tonne of chickpeas, which produced an hour of very unhelpful farting later, and I decided to walk east.

Beirut isn't a terribly easy walking city, you see. There's the odd proper pedestrian crossing in the city centre, with actual lights, green men and so on, but mostly you just have to throw yourself across the road. Plenty of eye contact with drivers. No hesitation or changes of pace. I'd recommend Naples for practice.

And the cars tend to park right across the pavements, perpendicular to the road, so you just have to walk out into the street all the time. All the bloody time. And there's big cracks and holes everywhere. But not as much shit as you might fear, because only a small number of folk seem to have dogs.

Everybody's very nice. Up to a point.

I eventually ran out of Beirut proper, and realised that I'd now crossed the whole city over the course of my stay, having taken a big walk the day before, when I'd strolled all the way through the centre and the west, up through Hamra and onto the Corniche, and back again. Which took ages. And I really enjoyed it. It's the sort of city you could grow to love very quickly. Many people do. Terrible pity I don't speak Arabic.

So I kept going east and crossed over the river, the *fleuve*, which is actually just a tiny trickle of water in the middle of a rather nasty big concrete channel, and found myself in Bourj Hammoud, which is very Armenian, unlike Mar Mikhael, which is only *quite* Armenian.

I had some rather strong coffee, and thought about the next day, and imagined I saw an immediate and present indignation on the faces of the men and women walking past, like they'd been huckled out of the Ottoman empire a week ago Tuesday and they were STILL bloody here.

Three

My neighbour, a tight-mouthed woman in her late thirties with loose-fitting beige slacks and a grey t-shirt bearing the words 'Friend. Mother. Dreamer.' banged on the glass of my apartment door, prompting me to crack off a thin shell of sleep, bounce onto my feet and catapult myself through into the roomy, bright and tastefully decorated living room, as I later repeated online in the guest review.

I was only a couple of feet away from the door, a second away from opening it, when she rat-tat-tatted again, even though she could plainly see through the frosted glass that I was right there.

- Good mo—

- Taxi is here.

- Taxi? What time is it?

- Eight o'clock. Taxi is here.

- Eight? My... In fact, that's my alarm going off just now. I agreed ten o'clock with the driver on the phone.

- No. Eight. Ten is too late.

- But I—

- I tell Aram you come down five minutes.

So... She must know the taxi driver. Yes. That made sense. I'd worked out the people here would use drivers they knew personally. Okay.

I hoped this Aram would let us stop for coffee somewhere once we were clear of the city and out on the road. He did, up in the hills, and it was exactly the sort of place I would have imagined, with red plastic seats and something I vaguely categorised as cake that I couldn't quite understand.

I felt a bit nervous when we crossed into Shia territory in the Bekaa

10

Valley. You could tell. All of a sudden, there was a succession of massive black banners with some shouty-looking Arabic writing on them, accompanied by shouty images of clerics.

- They have black, and they take also red, and green, and they take even yellow. Why they must take all the colours? Aram complained.

We got to the first checkpoint, and I whipped my shades off, following Aram's lead. A religious-looking chap leaned into the driver's window even as the glass was still going down, and attempted to interest Aram in some sacred DVDs. Aram offered a polite *wa alaikum salaam* and then declined the offer, and nothing bad happened. Like, getting chained to radiators, that sort of thing.

I spent a full two hours marvelling at Baalbek, and took loads of photos. And then when I went out the exit, I was suddenly reminded of the Gallowgate on match day, with the souvenir sellers punting green t-shirts and so on.

- And what did the t-shirts have written on them, then? I think you like telling me about that.

- Don't joke.

They had all the colours Aram was sad about – red, green, and most of all yellow, with the Hezbollah symbol on them, with that outline of a machine gun at the top, you know?

I'll take two, please, I said to the seller. One medium, one large.

Aram's taxi was safely parked round a couple of corners. If he caught me with a Hezbollah tee he'd surely dump me down a ravine with no hesitation. That much I had taken care to absorb from his conversation during the journey.

Both of them yellow? the guy asked,

And I said, Yes. And are you well today?

He gave me a big smile, and reached down into a bag and pulled out a USB stick, which he wrapped in the medium t-shirt, which he wrapped in the large t-shirt.

Aram got me back to Beirut via a meal stop in Zahlé, which he declared a 'good Christian town'. It was indeed very nice, a little like Fontaine de Vaucluse, and the food was gorgeous. I have rarely enjoyed any salad so intensely or copiously as their fattoush and whatnot.

The next morning I was on the shitter in the apartment for an hour.

Beirut airport: so many rounds of X-rays and security checks I lost count, and it took a good three hours to get through everything. Perhaps not surprisingly – it's fucking Beirut, after all.

Flight to Paris. Wee bit of time in Paris. All fine, without incident. I don't need to tell you about Paris – you know Paris. Lovely big Breton crêpes – *galettes*, strictly speaking – and some amazing modern Thai cuisine I hadn't been anticipating. Very nice.

Then the Eurostar. Whitehall, old-fashioned wood-panelled office, just how Whitehall offices might be reconstructed on a filmset. Hand over the USB stick. A nice hot coffee (on a proper saucer, eh) offered condescendingly like I'm some Jock sapper who usually slurps stewed tea from a billy can, pat on the back, train home up the road, cheque in the bank.

Four

Okay, so, BANG! and we go back to the 1980s.

Back to school for Gavin. Upon which a few observations, as a sort of warm-up, before we come to the singularly important career developments, which will happen in Cambridge.

Gavin's father was hellbent on accountancy.

Put another way, Iain Dougall Jamieson, born in 1939, was a living embodiment and proponent of chartered accountancy, such that any alternative life course for his and Anne Jamieson, née White,'s only child, a son, Gavin, would be considered not so much disappointing, or treacherous, or underachieving, as simply idiotic. Note, here, the overwhelming urge to consolidate one's family's class position without, crucially, even thinking about it. See also male privilege, white privilege, blah blah blah.

As a school pupil in one of the leafier tranches of Glasgow, Gavin sported, or more accurately was compelled to wear, a 'charcoal' blazer and a 'charcoal' and 'amber' (or 'frankly orange') tie (hence the said ties had always effectively come in Dundee United colours, predating the existence of Dundee United per se by a number of years), being the uniform of that primly suburban independent institution of primary and secondary education, Cauldbank College, inevitably *Cold Wank College* to its detractors.

Not to be confused with Calderbank, on the edge of Airdrie, where at least one bewildered new pupil typically gets taken at the end of August each year by less geographically astute parents.

Then, through to Edinburgh in time for senior school.

The opening observations on which are these.

1. The teachers had their various faults and peculiarities, but many of them were pretty good at teaching. They indisputably knew a thing or two, between them, about gerunds, quadratic equations, Operation Barbarossa, hepatic portal veins, the *Iliad*, Boyle's law, irregular Latin verbs, detour indices, metaphysical poetry, fractional distillation, proscenium arches and preceding direct objects. Things were learned, and attainment was high, via a peculiar combination of the Scottish and English examination systems.

2. They made you (boys) play rugby there. Half seemed to actually enjoy it. The other half could stop playing rugby after a few compulsory years, if (i) they were especially inept and/or (ii) they asked, or more accurately *beseeched*, the 'head of games', Mr Sarran, to be allowed to stop.

3. Gavin was not artful enough to play atrociously at rugby. It would have been better for him if he had managed this. If you systematically bungled enough passes and wussed out of all your tackles like a baby and didn't respond constructively to being shouted at, you got removed from the domain of rugby football as a drain on coaching resources and were henceforth given licence to doss about playing what the rest of the country would refer to as 'football', and not even on the proper playing fields but in the adjacent public park, with Mr Schatter, the pottery teacher. Opting for the less dextrous code, known condescendingly as 'soccer' by the school authorities, you could then relax on the field of play, because nobody would shout at you any more. In fact, you were suddenly at liberty to play so ineptly that it would almost be an insult to the professionalism of the football to fully inflate it.

Instead, and catastrophically, Gavin was mediocre at it, rugby. He made little genuine effort, but displayed a keen, earnestly strained face in order to avoid getting shouted at, in particular by Mr Lantry and Professor Stott, who were in charge of the third year's second practice, which provided the 3rd and 4th XVs. On the few hot days in late August or September, Gavin would stand disconsolately waiting for the next kick-off with an aching heart, wishing for nothing but the chilled Garvie's Apple Crush of youth. At least he was a forward, where you could spend quite a lot of the time vaguely shoving and being shoved, thus avoiding some of the more visible individual errors that come with being a back.

But this attainment of a level of borderline capability in and around the front and second rows of the scrum, while getting him off being

14

shouted at too frequently, still backfired, because he occasionally got selected, horrifyingly, for the 2nd XV at times of injury crisis.

Hence, picking a moment, Gavin found and approached Mr Sarran during one lunch break and begged him to add his name to the list of clod-hopping dolts who couldn't or wouldn't embrace the institutionally central and proper activity bequeathed to the domain of chaps by William Webb Ellis in, it is reckoned, 1823.

I'm just forgetting about that 1, 2, 3 numbering I started off above. Lost it, really. Sorry.

I'll try some bullet points in a minute.

Even north of the border, there were a few places where you could find teachers who were SO ENGLISH / POSH that they called it 'rugger' without irony.

Also:

- aspirations to drink Pimm's, attend Oxbridge
- becoming a lawyer, chartered accountant, or some such
- only later discovering the bonus world of auditing, like a hand-rubbingly thrilling secret
- offering the comment 'Yah, it's a useful skill to have' when discussing the prospect of learning to drive, like you're clever for spotting this, never in a million years contemplating that you, or indeed anybody, might ever use this skill to make a living by doing deliveries in a lorry or van, or driving a bus or a taxi, or anything like that
- having a special word like 'Transitionbobs' or 'The Upheaval' or *Bastardi* to designate the first year of senior school, which is primary 7 in Normal Scotland
- similarly, calling homework something else wanky, like *prep, doovers* or *chores*
- thinking Greek is a thing, and incomprehension when asked if you mean modern Greek
- Oh, here's one, Jesus…. CALLING FELLOW PUPILS BY THEIR SURNAME, IF YOU CAN EVEN BELIEVE THAT, LIKE YOU'RE IN THE ARMY OR A NIGEL MOLESWORTH BOOK.

- To be clear, Cauldbank wasn't quite as posh as that, was it?

- That's quite correct. At Cauldbank, you thought it was uncool if you didn't have some degree of proper Glasgow accent; once I got through to Edinburgh, though… Well. What can I say?

- I can imagine. But… You haven't said very much about the primary phase.

- No... Well, I suppose one thing everyone remembers: it was the early 80s, so people would call you a 'spastic' in response to any and every episode of reduced dexterity. All the time. I'd like to think I didn't do that myself. We were told to stop it, eventually.

- Indeed... And what else?

- What do you want? The invention of the Wispa and other 80s confectionery nostalgia?

- Were you bullied at all, Gavin?

- Bullied? Is that one of your stock questions? Yes. Briefly. Thanks for asking. My bully was called Tubby Wilson – and he was, objectively, quite tubby. Now, he was a proper bully – an old-fashioned, regulation bully, if you will – who patrolled the playground, actively and demonstrably bullying people. He would approach his victims with "Hey, you!" or something assertive like that. After a while you learned what his favourite sweets and crisp flavours were, and you started to ensure they were no longer your favourites and you didn't really mind not getting to eat most of them, and that would work pretty well, at least for avoiding pain.

It was possible he was a bully precisely because he looked a bit tubby and his name was Tubby, yet he didn't want to be tubby or acknowledged to be tubby. I can see that now.

At the age of 10, Gavin, being reasonably bright,

- Third person again now? Are you feeling uncomfortable about something?

- At the age of 10, Gavin, being reasonably bright, and above all compliant, was appointed a monitor. Being a 'monnie' at that school was like being in the Child Gestapo, in that it gave one powers to enforce rules and haul younger children up the stairs to the heidie's office for punishment, which was occasionally ruthless and physical.

Of course, this was mostly for trivial transgressions, such as encroaching by a few yards over an invisible line into a forbidden section of the school grounds.

It happened again at the end of senior school in Edinburgh, at the age of 17. That is, being appointed a school monitor. Only decades later did Gavin start to wonder how much psychological harm might have stemmed from his having 'arrested' miscreants for such diverse transgressions as jumping the tuck shop queue, skipping morning assembly or enjoying a cigarette.

Five

- The fact you've paused here is interesting.
- Is it? Well, the thing is, I could go on and on about school, and tell you all sorts of random things and recollections, or I could try and go through what it was like in chronological order, but I don't think I can quite be bothered. It would all mean something to me, but I can't see it would have any relevance. Can you?

I could still entertain my old friends with my impression of Mrs MacSnell that time she found the plastic egg full of daisies that someone had catapulted over from the other side of the chemistry labs, or I could tell you about how Zoe Blair ran into the dining hall shouting "There's a boy locked in the woodwork room!" when we were all having our jumbo sausages, and there was pandemonium, because everyone wanted to run out and have a look, and our class was especially excited, because we knew that Malcolm Prendergast was stuck in there going hungry over the split double period, lashed to the workbench—

- I'm sorry?
- Despite what we in these enlightened times might identify as an unacceptable fire risk, Mr Carruthers had tied him, M Prendergast, by the wrists to a clamp on the side of the workbench over lunchtime, because he'd tried to shove a triangular offcut of wood into Jane Knox's mouth, which was because she'd called him a silly little dick, which was because he'd started spinning hacksaws up into the air like a juggler. If memory serves, he poured a pot of honey into Sally Ruthven's hockey bag the day after for some reason or other. No wonder, though. People do irrational things when they have their agency taken away from them.

As I say, though, there'd be no point.
- Okay. So, university, then. You went to university.

- Yes. Cambridge.
- Cambridge?
- Yes.
- Which college did you attend?
- King's. You know I know your sister, don't you, Leena?
- I'm… I'm sorry?
- I know your sister.
- Please don't call me by my name in this context. We agreed on that.
- You're obviously about to ask which sister I'm talking about. June. But we'll come on to Chloe later.
- What? You've met June? You *know* her? And… And Chloe, too?
- I know both your sisters, Leena. I know them both intimately.
- That's… I… I don't think that's possible. I'd really rather you—
- June's lovely. Quite unique. You're blushing. She's very popular – we both know that – and very independent, and I think that's why she's so popular, and men are fascinated by her. She's good looking too, of course. Although, not in a… You know what I mean: *library* attractive, more than *disco* attractive. They're strongly attracted to her, are men. And we got talking a few times, and then we went off and had quite the best weekend together.
- Um… Right… When?
- A few years back. We're only just Facebook friends these days, but that weekend, my god. It was just perfect.
- You told me you weren't on Facebook.
- God, no – well, not using my real name, obviously.
I'll tell you about that weekend in a bit, anyway.
- You're not going to tell me about it now?
- Em… No. You asked about university.
- This isn't f…
- What?
- You're doing this deliberately. Hitting me with something very personal directed at me. While simultaneously making out that I'm in charge of getting you to tell me about your personal life, asking the questions and prompting you, Gavin.
- Well, yes. You're in charge of this questioning. You're questioning me.
- Tell me about my… No… Just go ahead and tell me about university.
- You want to know about me and your sisters, obviously, but it's hardly professional to ask about that, I'd say.
- What is this, Gavin?
- It's you asking me about me, counsellor. I'm paying you.

18

- Not strictly true. Don't say that again.

- Don't say what again?

- Don't waste your time trying to gaslight me. It's tedious and pointless. Don't be an arse.

- I *beg* your pardon.

- I said this might not be easy, Gavin. Perhaps I was telling myself that, too.

- You didn't say this would be either easy or not easy. Did you?

- I'm assuming you're going to tell me about university next. King's College Cambridge. Whatever you have to tell.

- Well, yes – it's crucial to everything.

- And if and when I invite you to tell me about my sister – my sisters – all you need to worry about is telling your story. If I then have to go and talk to them, that's my affair.

- Your family affair.

- Exactly. This, on the other hand, is about you.

Six

King's.

I enjoyed going down for interview. I didn't make a terribly good job of it, though, that was pretty obvious at the time. It was cold. Cold and crisp. December. I really liked it, in fact. Including the train journey. There was the most wonderful thick frost everywhere going down through East Anglia, and the sun breaking up patches of fog. I had to change at Peterborough and then Ely, where I wandered down to the river next to the station for a bit between trains. I'd love to go back and visit the place properly. The cathedral and so on. Twee little cafes or bookshops or whatever.

The interview was depressing, the more I think about it. I've no idea about now, but languages degrees back then were basically literature degrees, and I failed to convince them I was terribly interested in all that. I couldn't be bothered faking it.

And she gave me a row for wearing a thin jacket and no jumper or coat or gloves or hat on such a cold day.

Wrong crowd. They'd have been well impressed at Newcastle Poly, I bet.

I stepped out of the interview – or the second interview, in fact: it was in two parts – and it took me a while to find someone who was doing the same course as the one I was applying for, but I eventually did, when I sat down for lunch in their canteen, and she wasn't especially chatty... But then she asked me a question about my spoken Russian, and I...

- Yes?

- Well... This is where it gets interesting. I'm a bit hazy about what I said to her. I think I actually spoke about the French part of my interview instead, about how the tutor had the strongest Welsh accent I've ever heard.

- In French?

- Exactly. Which had surprised me.

Anyway. The girl I was speaking to didn't have long – she was just finishing her lunch before heading off for a lecture – but only about a minute after she left, and me still trying to get through my rubbery lasagne I think it was, this woman comes over, late 30s or 40ish, I'm guessing a tutor of some sort, and sits down, and says Gavin, and I say yes, and I try and say something else polite to introduce myself, and then she says...

Well, the thing is, I'd been fantasising, I have to admit to you, about how at some point in my final year I'd get a tap on the shoulder on the street somewhere in central Cambridge and I'd get The Question. You know what I'm talking about?

- I think so.

- And the last thing I expected was to get it on my interview day.

So, she sits down, obviously doesn't say what her name is, and asks me, "Perhaps, in three years' time, you might consider joining the civil service. You could have a job... an interestingly *different* job. Do you think that's a possibility?" And I say yes, basically, and she does two things. First, she tells me there might be a few little simple tasks I could get started with, and hands me an A4 sheet of code words – phrases, abbreviations and so on – and tells me to memorise them as soon as possible and then burn the paper or eat it or something, and the second thing she does is give me an envelope with £500 in tenners and I could have a hundred times that when she next sees me if all goes well.

Which wasn't quite true.

- Wow... And so... You got into Cambridge, then?

- God, no.

- You told me you attended King's College Cambridge.

- Yes. I "attended" an interview there. Only thing was, as I've already indicated, I made a bit of an arse of it. I got as close as you can get to getting into Cambridge without actually getting in. As soon as I saw the admissions tutor's thin envelope on the doormat I knew I'd be matriculating at the obviously less august but practically more helpful Edinburgh Hermiston University instead.

Seven

I was nervous.

I was nervous about being so near the heart of the Russian State – I was literally just across the river from the Kremlin – but also, in a funny way, nervous about being on British territory too. I had it in my head that the embassy was home turf, yet simultaneously an alien place. I was jittery as well as relieved, at the same time. A bit surreal.

I imagined I was about to speak to some posh guy, or some posh woman, and it turned out to be both, in that order.

The bloke was only there to do the initial admin stuff with me. It was the woman who was in charge of the matter at hand.

Their coffee was quite poor, but they put a plate of McVitie's Digestives in front of you, which is exactly the sort of thing that makes you cry with homesickness and forces you to throw your weeping face onto Her Britannic Majesty's consular bosom, and co-operate.

- But you were going to co-operate anyway, even without the biscuits.

- Of course. It literally didn't occur to me not to co-operate. I loved the biscuits, and I had three. No. Four.

So, she tells me to keep studying hard, try and make a few Russian friends and get my accent as good as possible by imitating them, and get my stresses right, and she asks me about my dissertation, and she's quite pleased, because it's political, and I'd be interviewing some highly placed journalists and a fairly high-up official or two at the Moscow Mayor's Office.

Anyway, she tells me I'll be more of a delivery boy than James Bond, basically, and it's just a matter of going places and getting files, letters, documents or computer disks, as it tended to be back then, and bringing them usually back to London, or sometimes to an embassy somewhere or other, and the money was pretty good and I would get to travel and claim my expenses back, and as long as I didn't drop the thing into a river or let baddies steal it off me I'd be fine. And she explained a bit more about the codes and so on.

You're frowning. Yes – there's loads of stuff that's sent via encrypted channels online these days – most stuff, I suppose – and then on the hard-copy side there's some things that aren't so sensitive – well, still *rather* sensitive – that can be sent by diplomatic bag, which I could theoretically get told to do myself, but they say they don't like mixing up the diplomatic bag carriers with the secret runners, like me, because obviously your name pops up at the airports and so on, and they'd wonder what you're doing going about without a diplomatic bag all of a sudden.

Or, conversely, with a bag.

You see?

Okay, so the first exercise was a balls-up, but it was only an exercise.

- What happened?

- First of all, I should explain that the embassy people gave me two sealed envelopes with instructions. The envelopes were numbered 1 and 2, but in code, which that week was Q and W. The notes were written in phonetic Doric, which tends to throw the Russians off.

- The British embassy has a resident Doric speaker?

- Sure. He's called Neil, and they keep him down in the basement. Butteries are brought down to him on Mondays and Thursdays.

So I opened up the first envelope when I was back in my hotel. I was supposed to intercept a tour-guide in a Cossack suit wandering around the Kolomenskoye Estate and have a bit of Q and A with him, but it didn't work out. Not much of a story: I just couldn't find the bugger. I was absolutely crapping it, though – I thought I'd be in big trouble. I assumed I'd gone to the wrong part of the grounds.

They weren't that bothered. In fact, it was their fault it didn't go right, not mine. The guy had slept in or got the day wrong, or was having an affair with a student – that was it – and wasn't getting paid enough to get out of bed. Or something like that. Back in my hotel I got a brief phone call from someone who said they were an embassy official, obviously speaking from a taxophon somewhere on a busy street – one of those shitty payphones, you know? – and they had a weird squeaky voice like a talking dog holding a wet hanky over the receiver. But anyway, I opened the second envelope, which told me where to go next, and when, and what to do when someone wearing a t-shirt with 'Crazy. Softly. Sleepy.' written on it asked me for 'the maths,' which made no sense at the time, obviously.

- Sorry – I've just realised: Q and W for 1 and 2? As in the start of QWERTY, is that?

- Oh! Very good. I'm impressed. Note taken.

Okay... So I think it was a couple of days later. I hadn't been up to that part of town before. I got out the metro at Dinamo station, next to the stadium obviously, and I saw him at the top of the escalator: unremarkable young guy, but I spotted the badge on his rucksack straight away. The four-leafed clover.

I came up behind him. You support Celtic? I said.

He turned round, as if surprised, revealing, to confirm, his horribly designed brown, yellow and smashed ivory t-shirt bearing the enigmatically bland 'Coffee and Living' in swishy pink lettering, and—

- Hang on – you said it was "Crazy, Softly—

- I know. I know. That one comes later.

So, we proceeded to buy tickets from a little booth at the corner of the stadium, for a little less than £2 at the official exchange rate – but this being the 90s, the price was enough to make this semi-final unaffordable for most would-be fans, keeping the attendance down to a paltry 13,000.

The ninety minutes of play were reasonably absorbing, producing a Dinamo victory over their greatest rivals, Spartak, by a goal to nil. The fans were mainly congregated in their respective groups towards one end, close enough to bellow at each other but far apart enough to avoid brawling. The Dinamo fans made disparaging remarks about Spartak's connection with meat and derived foodstuffs, notably kebabs, drawing on the club's food factory origins; the Spartak supporters condemned the Dinamo fans as 'filth,' given their police and KGB/FSB connections. The chanting and shouting were great for vocab.

My new young friend, Dima, explained that he was in fact a Torpedo fan, but had been tempted by a cup semi-final within easy reach of where he lived, and went on to stress that he would always favour Dinamo over Spartak, before recounting how Torpedo's most bitter rivals in the capital were in fact CSKA, and that some quite decent fights between CSKA supporters wearing Rangers tops and Torpedo fans with Celtic tops were a niche yet current feature of life for the city's young male *fanatiki*.

I asked him if he had any information for me, and he just laughed and shook his head, which made my heart sink. I wasn't expecting that response.

Then he started to explain: Wednesday, he said.

Wednesday? I said.

Yes, Wednesday you meet me again. This time you come to Torpedo stadium. Our stadium. In evening. A league game – against Vladikavkaz.

Now I understood why I'd been booked into my hotel for six nights. Why I had to go through these hoops, with so much downtime in between, was beyond me, but I had been warned that these operations sometimes involved more than one stage, and a bit of waiting.

So…

- Yes?

- You've not asked me if Dinamo went on to win the cup.

- Did Dinamo Moscow go on to win the Russian Cup?

- Yes. Against Rotor Volgograd in the final if I remember rightly. I'm trying to think whether it was on penalties. I'm not sure. I'd have to look it up.

- I didn't ask you, because I don't care. Why would I care?

- Hmm.

Anyway. So, that Wednesday came around soon enough, and I made my way to the Streltsov stadium, which isn't terribly big, but it's in quite an open, green part of the city, and it was a very pleasant summer evening, with sunshine washing down the whole pitch nicely. Lots of trees around.

Dima was clearly proud of his team, but he didn't really say very much, so I didn't get much of a feel for what made him tick, why Torpedo was such a special club, the importance of camaraderie and faith in the power of socialism among the ZiL factory workers, etcetera etcetera. You know Torpedo was originally the ZiL works team, yes?

The home crowd grew extremely unhappy, because Spartak Vladikavkaz played rather well, and scored some goals. In fact, they went on to win the league, for the only time ever, and you won't be the slightest bit interested to know that they went on to lose to Rangers in the preliminary round of the Champions League in the latter part of that year, by which time, if I remember correctly, they had changed their name to Alania Vladikavkaz, a fact which I am sure will concern you not one jot.

So, tempers were wearing thin. If you ask me, I think a lot of the home fans were rather dehydrated. Quite a few did have Celtic tops on, funnily enough… and they were angry, and my fear that things could kick off at any moment was realised, I'm afraid.

The thing was, there were a few fans, away fans, who'd come up from the Caucasus, and there didn't seem to be any segregation. And one of them, buoyed up by Vladikavkaz having scored two goals, shouted out something like, "Come on, lads, let's make it three!" which was fair enough, but arguably a bit stupid when you're surrounded by hundreds of dehydrated Muscovites. Some of whom were wearing t-shirts with 'Hooligan' on them, with gun sights in the two Os. Note the ambiguous cross-over with the far-right imagery there.

So anyway. A brawl started. *Draki*, as they would say, with a twinkle in the eye – Russian youths unfailingly have a twinkle in the eye when recounting tales of *draki*. Dima and I found ourselves on the edge of it, and he had to parry a couple of flying fists, while I started to shout out things like "Come on lads, calm down, eh!" and "There's no need for this," like some preposterous foreign wanker.

So then the OMON – their Belarusian counterparts made internationally famous more recently, by the way, for bundling folk into vans in Minsk – they turn up with their balaclavas on and pick half a dozen of the most fighty young lads, take them away, and have half an hour with them, after which they are returned to the main stand, looking a bit pale and shaky and quiet as they resume their places.

After the said stramash, things were calm, if melancholy. A 3-1 away win, if I recall.

At the end, it was all pretty orderly considering what had happened earlier: a few thousand people slowly funnelling off from the side of the stand down to the start of a track leading back to the main road. A bit of chat, a bit of resigned good humour after the defeat – and I had to remind myself that many of these good people would consider fighting as a perfectly routine bit of match-day fun. Still, I had a nervous feeling, like anything could happen in the next half-hour, to quote Commander Shore.

- Sorry?

- Sorry. Never mind that. So, Dima and I are part of that crowd leaving the stand, and he's asking me various questions about Celtic and Scottish football, and then he looks up ahead of us and it's like he's seen a ghost or something. He almost stumbles, and the people behind us knock into him and swear, so we keep going, but it's like his legs have turned to jelly.

It's quickly clear who's put the shits up him: this big tall guy with short blonde hair a good way up ahead, with his cold eyes elevated up above everyone else's heads, like a periscope, waiting, facing into the oncoming tide of exiting punters, and there's already nowhere else for Dima (and therefore me) to go than straight towards him.

And yet I feel calm now – completely calm – because I know Dima's in some sort of trouble or under some sort of pressure, not me, and it can't possibly affect me and I don't care.

There's no great subtlety about the questioning, so I'm able to follow the conversation:

- Where's the package?

- What? I don't have it today.

- You said tonight, at the end of the game, and here we are. Which pocket is it in? You want me to turn you upside down? Or why not just give me your coat? Who was it who gave you that coat in the first place anyway?

- But you… you said the weekend. I don't have it on me!

Fast forward through a bit more of this, lots of pointless repetition, on one side the threat, on the other side the terror, the waiting for it to stop and the desperate hope for a reprieve.

And the fascinating thing for me, of course, is that Dima appears not to be in on it at all.

- "In on it?"

- Yes. So, in hindsight I let the poor wee guy suffer for far too long, because he was genuinely afraid he was going to get... I don't know what exactly, pummelled or chibbed or whatever. Him and the big blonde guy weren't exactly new acquaintances, I don't think.

Anyway, it went on like this for a bit, and it got to the point where your big man says what I would probably translate as "For the last time, where's the fucking package, you piece of shit?"

So, I finally open my mouth. And to tell the truth, I'm pretty rattled by now. The guy doesn't even glance at me, but I'm standing right there next to him, and god knows what this fuckass is capable of when he's angry.

"Actually, I've got it," I say. "I've got your package."

- You could have said that much earlier, couldn't you? This poor Dima fellow was clearly scared half to death.

- Look, I was proper crapping it myself.

- "Completely calm", you said a minute ago.

- Well, maybe I was for the first few seconds. But scary people scare me somewhat: I don't play games with the alpha males if I can possibly help it.

- Thanks for throwing me that psych bone, there, Gavin. Charitable of you.

- I obviously half-expected the big guy to respond with a "Who the fuck are you?" sort of thing, at which point I'd be in serious trouble, as in physically in trouble, but he sort of quietened down and said, "Okay, come on, show me," and pointed over to a row of trees and one of those... structures – you know, those metal telecoms cabinets or boxes or whatever they're called. It was big enough to hide behind – everything's bigger in Russia, as you know – so we ducked down, and I flashed him the code, not showing him the whole thing, but enough for him to recognise what it was.

So Big Man there, ducking down quite awkwardly – we were all crouching down with some difficulty, because the ground was pretty muddy – flashes a sort of half smile and unzips his nasty lime green tracky top and reveals his t-shirt underneath, which said what?

- 'Crazy. Softly. Sleepy.'

- Exactamente correcto.

- "Where is maths?" he asks. So I hand him the package – except there was no package, in fact.

- There was no package?

- There was no 'package,' as such, no. He just needed the code. And the codename for the code – the bit of paper with the code on it, in other words – was 'the package.' You see?

- Okay.

- Yeah… You know… I really did have the most super time with June that weekend we had.

- Sorry? June – my sister? Why are you suddenly talking about that again?

- Her French is… It really is beautiful. Effortless.

- And her Spanish?

- Totally fluent from what I could make out the couple of times I heard her, although mine's not up to that much, it has to be said, so I could never be the best judge.

Why do you ask?

- Why are you talking about her now, all of a sudden? We were handing over codes in Moscow a few seconds ago.

- So, we met in Brussels Central Station. Busy. Quite a confusing place, with the different staircases and the pissy underground corridors going off in various directions. Doesn't have a proper main concourse, like the Gare du Nord, say.

Anyway, she turns up, and makes the signal.

- Signal? For god's sake. You got my sister into all that… shit?

- She just touched her ear – not 'Hello Gavin' in semaphore or something.

So I give her mine, and she—

- Your signal? Which was?

- Em… Sort of pretending to swat a fly on my left arm. She laughed at that – and my god, that smile—

- Where did you go? Fine dining? Hotel?

- Okay. Okay. We got a train along to Liège, and—

- Did you stay in a hotel there? Did you sleep together?

- Yes. We stayed in a hotel. I mean, I don't know what you're expecting me to say, but yes. Not fancy – the hotel. Nice enough bedroom, but only a pokey wee bar just next to reception, and the locals were all in the place, wearing milk-bottle glasses and smoking and swilling wee glasses of Jupiler. City centre, anyway.

- So, you did sleep together?

- Look – I won't say we didn't sleep in the same… Yes: we slept together.

But I was going to mention her hair. And her eyes. My god! I still

28

can't say to this day who she brought to mind when I first saw her, but it was so—

- Most people say Sarah Michelle Gellar, if that helps.

- What? Oh... Oh god, yes, of course. Ha! I hadn't quite—

- You haven't quite been telling me the truth about this at all. You've no idea what she looks like. Come on: you can do better than this.

- She has a birthmark on the back of her left leg, about yay big, like a bat and ball.

- Ah...

- I don't know how I could know that other than having... Well... What?

- Just keep talking. Or don't keep talking. In fact, don't mind me at all, Gavin.

- Also, she hiccups violently if you feed her Blue Curaçao.

- That's true enough.

- Em... Well anyway. The meal was okay, not amazing, but I just love the way you can start a conversation with her about one thing, and she just takes it so much further and tells the most insightful, funny—

- What year was this?

- Em... I'd say... Yes: 2004.

- 2004?

- Yes.

- Right.

What about Chloe, then?

- What? The other sister already? Had enough of my June story, then? I hadn't even started! In the morning we decided to take a walk up that massive staircase, the Montagne de—

- Chloe. What about Chloe?

- Ah. Well. That's different.

Hmm...

Chloe... Well, the first time I met her was when she was staying at your aunt's house.

- What? That couple of months when she was living there? In Edinburgh?

- Yes. Restalrig. I was taking a stroll through Restalrig.

- Are you out of your mind? Nobody *takes a stroll through Restalrig*.

- Nonsense. I find it a refreshing area of the city to take a walk in. A good place to clear your head. Sometimes I take a bus out Craigentinny way and walk back into town, often via the eerie tranquillity of Lochend Park.

- What were you doing at my aunt's house?

- Nothing.

- Right…

- In that I was just walking past on one of my strolls. It was just some random residential street as far as I was concerned. So, I'm wandering along the road, trying to decide whether to walk all the way back to Waverley or get a bus, when this old Nissan Micra pulls up 20 or 30 yards in front of me, screeching to a halt, the whole bodywork shaking and rattling with music thumping out at top volume.

And this woman winds down the window. She looks rough as fuck, I'm telling you. Sweaty plain black t-shirt, grubby grey joggy bottoms. Maybe an alkie, I was thinking.

- You're talking about my aunt here, Gavin.

- Your Auntie Ruby, yes, obviously. And she says—

- She's never mentioned you. Not once. And Chloe certainly hasn't.

- That's because I told them both not to.

- Aye, right. And how could you see her "joggy bottoms" anyway? She hadn't got out of the car.

- For goodness' sake, she got out of the car a few seconds later.

So, anyway, she says something towards the flat up on the first floor, presumably for your uncle to hear, but you couldn't… I couldn't possibly hear what it was, because at this point she still had Ob-La-Di, Ob-La-Da belting out of the car's sound system at full blast. Then she finally switches the radio off and gets out the car (see?), and she shouts "Danny! Danny! Fuckin bags! Fuckin petrol! Get yer arse oot here!"

- That's Ruby.

- Yes. And at the same time, I notice there's someone… a beautiful face looking out one of the bedroom windows. And I don't know what I'm thinking, but she's looking at me, and I sort of nod, as if to say Come on, let's go for a walk while your mother (as I wrongly assumed she was) calms down.

- You didn't know it was my aunt at this point. Really?

- I didn't know about *you* at this point. Really.

I'd already crossed over the road. I slow down, pretending to check stuff on my phone, and your aunt briefly bellows something else as she goes into the close but then nothing happens for a minute, so I get a cigarette out and take ages to light it.

- You smoke?

- Only for those situations when I need a crucial extra 30 seconds for street surveillance etcetera.

And just as I light it and start to move off down the opposite pavement very, very slowly, I finally hear Chloe's voice saying to her aunt, I'm just going *out*, auntie—out for a wee walk. I'll get milk and fags from the shop on the way back, okay?

And she crosses over the road, but I keep going along the pavement round the corner until I'm out of sight of the flat, behind that big hedge – you know where I mean?

- Yes.

- She soon catches me up, and we start walking around the streets, and eventually go into the park.

- Feed the ducks, did you?

- We didn't have anything for them.

So, we dated for about two months, I'd say.

- Woah... You are... kidding me, Gavin.

- You almost said 'fucking kidding me' – you can if you like. Don't be constrained by our having this conversation in an office.

- Okay, Gavin. You are kidding me the fuck on here.

But that's fine – it's all part of this thing... so carry on. Tell me all about it.

- Do I have to?

- No. Only if you want to. It's up to you. As ever.

- Because I don't really want to, actually. It was nice for a while – a good few weeks – quite gentle, and settled-feeling, even though we only started to talk about moving in together in the longer term... As in, further in the future some time. It's not as if we were ever going to shack up straight away. It's not like she was actually desperate to get out of your Auntie Ruby's place, although I sure as hell would have been.

- You realise why she was living there, then? You know about our mum's operation?

- Oh, yes – Chloe did mention that, yes.

- You know nothing, Gavin. It was my dad who was having an operation, followed by quite a long recovery in hospital; my mum was away on her orgasm tour of Central America at the time.

- Right. But the thing is, Chloe started talking more and more about what sort of house she wanted us to share some time down the line – as in house, not flat, note – and I was reluctant at first, but then warmed to the idea, and the happier I got with the thought, the more I felt closer to her and then...

- Not surprisingly, I know nothing about this. But anyway. Go on.

- And then, it sort of switches over, and it's me talking about getting a place together, not her. And it's me thinking about what we want and what we can afford. She says a semi would do fine, not fussed about where exactly; I'm fantasising about some interwar or 1950s detached nesting-home with a soft green garden, maybe in Linlithgow, or Queensferry, or Corstorphine, or up towards the Braid Hills, or—

- No chance.

- No chance? How do you know?

- Because she's my sister, for god's sake. And I can't help noticing, more to the point, that you're not together now. She gets cold feet. As soon as cohabitation becomes a serious possibility, she slams on the brakes. She absolutely needs her own space. Unshared. As I guess you found out. You'll have been the... fifth guy in that position, I think it must be.

- And money. I'd have considered Bearsden in an ideal world, but do you think I could actually afford a gaff somewhere like that?

- I honestly don't know, but I suspect you just about could.

- And then came the threats.

- Threats?

- Best not talked about.

- What threats?

- I'd rather not.

- Fine. I'd rather not know anyway. You mention something juicy, hook me, then say nothing more about it. All noted.

[*silence*]

- What's this: are we finished on the whole Chloe thing already?

- I think so.

- Okay. For starters, I can tell you that all of that crap about both of my sisters is... Just that: total crap. As you surely must know, June has been a hotel receptionist in Montevideo for many years, and in the year you say, 2004, I'm pretty sure she wasn't in Europe at any stage at all.

- *Pretty* sure, you say?

- Yes. God knows who you found out that stuff about her from, but somebody, some pal of hers could have told you any or all of it.

- Like, when you and June got home from school when you were 8 or 9 or whatever, you would take a packet of Opal Fruits and cut them all up into little quarters and mix them up in a bowl and call it 'salad' and eat them one tiny bit at a time.

- Happy days.

- Did Chloe not like Opal Fruits? It surprises me she was never interested in that delicacy.

- She did Digestives and Rich Tea, initially with a glass of cold milk, before developing her Nescafé habit.

- Hmm. You know, I've just thought, I suppose I should be telling you about my dreams and so on. You must get into that all the time in your work.

Well?

- There's no point in this whatsoever. But if you're going to tell me some coded thing via an invented dream you never had, you're going to do that. However, I could do with a toilet break first.

Eight

I woke up laughing the other morning. Literally woke up laughing.

I wish someone had been there to see it. It would have looked comical, I bet. Me, flailing around my bed, giggling like an idiot. My hot water bottle making slopping, gurgley noises as I thrashed around, trying to get it away from me, like some warm, intemperate fish. I was sweating and red with the heat of it. It had been that cold when I'd gone to bed the night before. When the wind blows strong enough, it gets through the bottom of the window frame and... Sorry: that's not very interesting.

- How can you wake up laughing?

- Has that never happened to you? Obviously it was a dream, but when I woke up, the way I thought of it was that I'd had an amazing idea for a comedy sketch in my sleep.

So, it's about a restaurant called QINETICK BRUNCH HITTING, which is what the big sign says above the door, white on red, in the same font as those Quick hamburger joints you get in France. Although we don't see the exterior at first.

In the first scene, you can see a few tables, four maybe, everyone looking apprehensive and scared. One diner has her face down on the table, holding onto the edge, trying not to hyperventilate, others are sweating, looking all around them, quite a few shaking in terrified anticipation, peering nervously every few seconds at the kitchen doors.

Then they all look up, because they can hear the sound of what seems to be a big stone rattling down the long metal pipe that runs the length of the sloping ceiling, opening out through a trumpet-shaped hole around half way along the table. A really big baked potato wrapped in greaseproof paper and string tumbles out of the end of the tube and falls onto the centre of this woman's plate, cracking it into three pieces, and the string comes

34

apart revealing the filling of coleslaw and beans. She screams. She calms down after a few seconds, though, and she's at least relieved the filling's not something else, like coronation dog food, or rat. And that the potato didn't land on her lap or her head. She looks around at the other diners and they nod kindly, prompting her to eat and enjoy her potato. The cutlery shakes in her hands.

Next thing, a waiter bursts out through the kitchen doors, which the diners had taken their eyes off for a minute, bearing a massive dish of scalding hot gnocchi in some sort of creamy pink sauce. Once he's out of the kitchen the waiter actually speeds up, breaking into a sprint as he heads for the table. So, when he puts it down to serve it he's having to come to a sudden stop, and because of this violent deceleration he spills most of the gnocchi and sauce over the table and nearly onto the lap of the recipient diner, who screams No, please no! and instinctively stands up to avoid the incredibly hot sauce, which cascades onto his chair. But as soon as he gets up, the maître d', who's got a terrifying long toothy face and is wearing a horrible shiny purple polyester suit, appears out of some strangely narrow elevator doors and shouts Do not stand up! You cannot leave the table!

The diner, disappointed and afraid, sits down on the hot gnocchi and sauce that have pooled on his seat, thus making a terrible mess of his trousers. He turns to, we presume, his wife, sitting to his left, and says:

(*Californian, nasal*): Feels like I shit myself, Gloria. In fact – I *have* shit myself!

EXT. Cut to a customer with her arm in a sling, getting let out. A different waiter holds the door open for her and says, "You can now go."

Then, as the camera pans out, he looks at the queue of half a dozen or so people outside, some of whom have crutches and eye patches. "Regulars, aye?" This waiter has a mixed Mediterranean-Scottish accent.

INT. For a second, we get a shot of all the diners looking towards the kitchen doors, to which we cut. Through them comes the same head waiter who had brought out the gnocchi earlier, pointing a bazooka at the diners. We hear screams and farts.

"Who ordered profiteroles?" the maître d' shouts, in a rather annoying, piercing voice, with some stupid sort of made-up accent. "Gladys? You order this?"

Gladys puts her hand up: "Aye, it is me, I ordered them." Immediately, she gets a set of four profiteroles shot at her head out of the bazooka, with very satisfying *plap!* sound effects. Close-ups of the mingling blood and cream running down her temple as she lies unconscious on the floor, her head next to a table-leg.

EXT. Pan out and up so that we can see the full restaurant sign for the first time. After a long pause, 15 seconds or something, a male diner with a whole trout strung round his neck in a net bursts out of the door shouting "Mercy!" followed two seconds later by a waitress. Close-up of her head and shoulders as she shouts Halt! You cannot leave. Come back immediately. Sir! Sir! You cannot leave – you are a signatory!

Pan back and down to reveal the harpoon gun she is holding. We hear a few running footsteps, indicating that the diner with the fish is attempting to flee. She fires. We hear and see the chord uncoiling and then the dreadful sound of the harpoon finding its target in the man's back, out of shot obviously, and his mortal screams.

Well?
Did you like that?
Any comments at all?

All right.
I went back to Moscow again after a year or so. It was nice to revisit some old haunts, but the place was changing really quickly, it being the late 90s, and I was disappointed that not all the street kiosks that had been there the year before were the same, if they were there at all. The 'Bavarian hot dog' lady had gone, and I was particularly sad about that.

I was told one morning to pack a suitcase for a few days, and then got instructions to go for a meal at my favourite Georgian restaurant. Frankly, Leena, that's the best thing about this job: you have to meet people a lot, and it very often involves dining out at places with quite nice food. God, I used to love that.

The thing about Elbrus... the restaurant in Moscow, not the mountain—

- Yes, I got that, thanks.

- It didn't have an alcohol licence back then, so the system was that when you went to hand over your coat to the 103-year-old *garderob* woman, you asked "Is there any wine available?" and she would say, if the district police chief was dining there that evening, as he did at least once a week, "I'm afraid you have to bring your own alcohol, sir, as we do not have a licence," in which case you'd have to dash out once you'd placed your order and grab a bottle of Hungarian from one of those kiosks; or else she would say "Just a moment," which meant that the district police chief was not expected that evening, and she stooped down to some recess or cupboard and produced a dust-covered bottle with Georgian script on it, and then a corkscrew, and before you could offer to help, inserted the metal point into the cork and made an absolute hash of opening the bottle, her frail bony hand shaking more and more violently as particles of cork started flying up into the air – "Just a moment," she interjected, as if interrupting her own operations, and then you try and say "Please, let me take the—" and then she shrieks at you in anger – and at last the bottom half of the cork tumbles out, together with a splash of oddly translucent-looking red wine, and you try and carry the bottle as unobtrusively as you can to your table, drips pouring down your hand.

"Table for two?"

"Yes. I am expecting my companion any moment."

Eventually, Yuri arrives, and instead of saying Good evening or Hello, he just says Great! Splendid!

- This is all in Russian, I take it.

- Yes, yes. He says Great. Splendid. Super. And eventually takes his coat off, revealing a slightly creased 'The Best That Life Can Get' t-shirt, at which I nod, and say "How much did that t-shirt cost you? Twenty dollars?" and he says "No. Ten dollars." At which point we can turn our attention to the menu.

Obviously we get stuck into the *khachapuri* straight away, and it's really nice. Cheese-bread, you'd call it, I guess. Thick and round – I later learned it can come in different shapes and sizes, too. The wine's just fine, in case you're wondering.

Just before the pudding arrives, he hands me a train timetable under the table, looks at my hair and Western style of glasses, and advises me to pretend to be Latvian when I go along to the Kievsky station, to avoid having to pay the Intourist rate for my ticket. He tells me to take the train going at the time he's circled on the timetable, and no other. He then offers me a five-minute course on how to speak Russian as badly as I already do, but with a Baltic accent. He goes on to tell me who to speak to when I get to Odessa station, but doesn't really explain anything else.

There's a hitch, though. Because of the channels this particular mission is going through, or more to the point the channels it's *not* going through, I have to hang around in Moscow for quite a while to wait for my visa to get in and out of Ukraine.

Not that there were the same tensions then between the two countries that there are today – far from it – it's just the way it was. They'd only been independent from each other for six or seven years back then, bear in mind. More on which later.

So, I had to get a *turistichesky vaucher* before I could get a visa. And those things took time to get hold of. I go into the Ukrainian embassy in Moscow, and I say "Can I get a tourist voucher please, for a visa?" and the lady at the desk doesn't say yes or no exactly, but just writes down an address on a bit of paper and gives it to me, with a note of the nearest metro station. I'm surprised, because it looks like a residential address.

I sit down in a café and get my map out, find the place and it's bloody miles out of town, a long walk or a couple of stops on a bus beyond the end of a metro line.

It's a slight pain in the arse. I get to the place towards five, worrying about when it might close, but it's okay – there's someone there. It's a ground-floor flat in a 20-storey tower block, as it turns out. I buzz and then knock, and I go in, almost wondering if I need to take my shoes off, as it's basically just someone's flat. There's an office desk in the living room, with a telephone and some papers on it, and a big map of Ukraine on the wall, which looks like it could have just been hastily tacked up there when I was approaching the building, and a man with glasses, sitting there. It's like some post-Soviet mockery of that office in the opening sequence in *The Prisoner* where McGoohan hands in his resignation to the baldy guy with the specs sitting at his… Never mind – sorry.

- No – I've watched *The Prisoner*. I know exactly what you mean.
- Okay.

So, I get my tourist voucher, being no more than a paltry handwritten receipt, effectively, in exchange for a particularly crisp $50 bill, with few words exchanged, apart from the irritating news that I now needed to wait five days before obtaining my actual visa from the embassy, hence the date on my train ticket for the day after that.

Speaking of which, when I went to the station to get the said ticket, I did rather well, I thought. I was quite rude and used my elbows and slurred my words so that they duly thought I was from Riga or something and not a westerner. I carefully avoided saying please or thank you or anything daft like that, and it worked: I got a ticket at the normal price.

Damned if I could ever pull that off again, though.

Anyway.

I have rather fond memories about that train journey, from Moscow to Odessa. Best part of 30 hours, if I remember rightly. I shared a six-man compartment with a man who resembled Tommy Boyd offof the Wide Awake Club, and his wee boy, who was learning English out of a Disney book, and a Soviet man in a dreadful grey and blue tracksuit who laughed at me contemptuously for choosing to read a book in English. We shared my plasticky baguette I'd brought with me along with their hard-boiled eggs and cucumber.

- Were you offered salt that they'd brought in a matchbox?
- I deduce from that question that you've done the Trans-Siberian.
- *Sovershenno verno*. Four years ago.
- Terribly dull journey, I hear. Yet at the same time an unmissable trip of a lifetime etcetera.

Now, Kiev, which we passed through, had something visibly wrong with its trees, because of Chernobyl, and there were farmers working on the land by the trackside using scythes. The toilet at the end of the carriage was very horrible after the first few hours. I don't remember much else. Uneventful journey overall, though.

You could see how all these until-recently-Soviet people were rather bemused by the border guards coming onto the train and checking everyone's *dokumenty*. Back in the 1990s, some people had new Russian or Ukrainian passports, while plenty others still had their old CCCP ones, which continued to be accepted as long as they were in date, I think.

Actually, I remember: Tommy Boyd laughed out loud when I mentioned having to go to the Ukrainian embassy in Moscow. The very idea of it had him in hysterics.

- Because it would seem to him like going to a Scottish embassy in London.

- Or even to a *Yorkshire* embassy in London, more like.

Anyway, I was met at Odessa station by an old Ukrainian chain smoker with gold teeth called David, who jabbered some comments about the weather and the trains always being half an hour late. He unzipped his crappy stained jacket and unbuttoned his long-unwashed cardigan, revealing his yellow t-shirt with 'Scratch my Love' in dark blue lettering, at which point I nodded and told him my favourite and least favourite varieties of *pirozhki*, upon which he directed me to the sellers of same and handed me a slip of paper.

I got a taxi to the address, which was a recently converted sanatorium, sometimes used for student halls, sometimes as a not-quite-officially recognised hotel.

You walk past a statue of Lenin reclining, reading a book and thinking about things, such as the great man might well have done when relaxing on a summer's day, and you then go into the most appallingly designed lobby, with sort of bulbous, multi-coloured glass things framed around what appeared to be a dance floor for Andropov-era students with awful clothes and perms.

When I pressed the elevator button I noticed a streak of dried blood at the bottom of the doors and entertained myself with different scenarios to explain it.

- Murder on the Dancefloor.

- Probably, I thought.

I put my things away in my room, which had a cracking view over the gardens and the Black Sea, and then knocked on the door immediately across the corridor.

A memorably busty if plain-faced—

- You're not doing yourself any favours with this, Gavin.

- A woman in her 30s opened the door and nodded at me, so I pulled up my jumper to reveal my

Not this button
Not this button
Not this button
Not this button
This button

t-shirt, and she did the same to reveal her new-looking black number, which had 'Bullshit Vacancias' written on it in white capitals.

We both nodded, and she told me where to go the next morning. I was getting closer to my target, but there were still more stages.

I proceeded the next day, after not so much a breakfast as a fruitlessly circular conversation about the de facto non-availability of breakfast facilities in the accommodation, to the famous Privoz market, as recently featured, you'll note, in Valeriy Todorovskiy's highly acclaimed *Odessa*.

Making my way, as instructed, to "the pig's head which is always to be found", which was indeed not difficult to locate, I kneeled down admiringly before it, prompting a few snorts of "*Turist!*" etcetera, and spotted the little plastic tag attached to its tongue. Memorising the four-digit number (to be recited later in combination with a well-known Russian tongue twister), I then made my way to the tram terminus, where there was a slight scene, in that a crowd of something like a hundred people were all waiting on the tram (which was a free service at this point, in fulfilment of the mayor's astonishing election pledge), and there was a certain level of consternation as the news was getting round that there was only one single carriage on that particular line, trundling along the length of the track and back again, with feverish disagreement and speculation about when it had most recently disappeared out to the edge of the city.

When it arrived 20 or 25 minutes after I'd got there, I tried to crowd in, but it wasn't quite possible, although I could see that if I threaded my arm between the two passengers in front of me to hold onto the pole inside and put my right foot on the footplate and put my left foot on my right foot, I might be alright.

The driver delayed her departure, and everyone started staring at me and shouting at me for a little while before I eventually realised the delay was because of me and my backpack blocking the driver's view from her wing mirror.

I handed my bag over, and the driver put it down at her feet. We set off. I admired the falling-to-bits factories and various other peculiar buildings, and as we got closer to the edge of town it got greener and really quite pleasant. My arm was aching like hell with holding onto the pole for several miles, and my cheeks were getting whipped by the bullrushes.

When we got to my stop I screamed PEREDAITYE POZHALUISTA RYUKSAK at the driver at the top of my voice, and then felt a bit embarrassed, because it was the last stop anyway.

It was a lovely relief to get off the thing. I crossed over the highway towards the shore of the *liman*, which is a sort of lagoon, separated from the Black Sea by a few miles. At that point it wasn't the nice beach I had imagined, but just a lot of big, sharp boulders, which made getting about rather difficult.

I was surprised at this point, because the Bullshit Vacancias lady had told me, after we'd started in Russian and then switched to English: "His name: Shirley Tempelhof." Now, at that point, I remember saying to her, "Right... Well, we would say, '*Her* name' if it's a woman." She had then repeated "Shirley - Ha ha ha!" and the two of us had suddenly become hysterical, and we ended up sitting down together on the bed in her room, and without warning she pulled out this little hip flask of *samogon* out of her jeans pocket, and I was incredibly turned on by the fact it was at her body temperature, and we just kept laughing non-stop as we started drinking, and then we started fucking like there was no tomorrow.

- Very James Bond.

- Yes, I suppose so. It got very sweaty.

- Did you take the opportunity to ask her about the bloodstain on the elevator doors?

- Yes! Ha ha! Yes, I did, in fact. She said "Oh yes, that was just a shoot-out between the local Dagestani mafia clans," so I'm like "Woah," and she's like "It was fine. They were very quick and then they went away. The cleaner managed to remove all the blood, except she forgot about elevator door."

So anyway, back to Shirley Tempelhof. She, or rather he, turned out to be a rather muscular Japanese man who had learned English with a strong Irish accent. Any doubts in my mind about her/his identity were eliminated by the fact he was duly holding a copy of Bulgakov's classic—

- The Master and Margarita?

- Yes. In conjunction with his wearing a sharply lettered 'Get Bent, Fuckstick' t-shirt.

- You're sure he wasn't an Irishman of Japanese heritage?

- No. We talked about it.

We then exchanged some lines from the famous opening scene of the novel.

- The Patriarch Ponds stuff?

- Yes... That's right!

- For goodness' sake, Gavin: you do realise woman can and do read books, too?

- Leena! Of course: it's just I didn't—

- Have you even read my CV? Look… just keep going, okay? And don't 'Leena' me – I've told you.

- Okay. So, after I give him the code number from inside the pig's mouth—

- And the tongue twister?

- Шла Саша по шоссе и сосала сушку.

- Classic.

- So, in combination with the number, it was 'Shla Sasha po shosse i sosala 2,170 sushek,' you see?

- Okay.

- Then he just says "Take the book," and he tells me to wait for him to leave, and I can take the tram after the one he gets on, and sorry in advance if it's a long wait, but "That's not my fuckin problem, dude," he says, which is slightly irritating.

Thing is…

Thing is, Leena, I want that memory to be associated with sunshine, and a place of great beauty, exotic not in any objective sense, but exotic for us, as westerners, with the bleak Soviet film-settery of the place. Somewhere in the middle of nowhere. A shoreline of sorts. A place where Odessites would go for a picnic.

- You said it was big sharp boulders everywhere.

- Yes… Well, you'd be able to have a picnic somewhere nearby. Just round the corner, probably.

But when I try and remember those glistening rocks, and the sun and blue sky and the water, and the peace and the lack of people around, I'm convinced it wasn't in the least bit beautiful. It still managed to be drab and shit.

- The post-Soviet space, Gavin.

- Speaking of which, it was a good 10 years before I went back to Ukraine, as it turned out.

You're looking blank, Leena.

- Am I?

- You're paying attention to all this?

- Of course. I'm in for the long haul today.

- How do you know this isn't going to continue into tomorrow?

- Oh, god.

- Look at this.

- What?

- You see this scar?

- You said he said "Take the book." So… What: was there something hidden in a secret compartment in the middle of The Master and Margarita?

- Oh, yes. That was exactly it: two USB sticks contained in decoy packs of Wrigley's chewing gum.

- Spearmint?

- No. One Doublemint; one Juicy Fruit.

- Nice.

- You see this scar?

- Umm…

- Just at the bottom of that rib. See?

- Oh yes.

- What if I told you my own grandmother viciously stabbed me with a meat fork, right there, when I was eight, on Christmas Day, and I had to be rushed to hospital?

- One of those two-pronged ones?

- Yes. As you can see.

- Maternal or paternal grandmother?

- Um…

- Oh, good grief! You hadn't even thought of that? You really do fall into it sometimes! You're making all this stuff up to shock me and distract me, all this random nonsense. Bluffing like a child half the time, regurgitating scraps of happenstance the rest of it.

- It's up to you to decide whether I'm making it up or not.

- Yes. I understand that perfectly, and you're not listening, least of all to yourself. And strictly speaking, it's not up to either you or me to *decide*; I can work it all out, or I can guess, and what you think about that – however much I get right and however much I get wrong – is up to you.

Nine

- Geneva. Now, that was the one time I actually got chased. Like, someone was literally chasing me through the streets, trying to steal my diskette.

- Russians? SVR?

- You do ask the right questions, Leena. Yes.

My contact at the airport told me to get myself to Sécheron station, which took very little time, and I even had a few minutes between trains at Cornavin to nip downstairs and grab a nice salty brezel. The woman on the platform at Sécheron identified herself by withdrawing a Kägi fret bar from the vending machine and throwing it at my head, which suggested she must have been given my description, including my decoy Leo Sayer wig.

Saying little—

- Did you eat the Kägi fret bar?

- Of course.

Saying little, we walked the short distance to the new headquarters building of the World Maritime Trade Council, stopping off at an Asian sandwich bar, where a family from Birmingham had set up a fine business selling the best chicken curry baguettes in the world. I complained I wasn't hungry, and my temporary companion looked at me like I was a complete idiot. We took our sandwiches along to a bench, and I lost myself in the creamy, spicy, chickeney world of my immaculate baguette for a few minutes, although I had to splay my legs wide apart to avoid the curry sauce dribbling out and making a humiliating, disgraceful mess on my trousers. She (whatever her name was) was clearly addicted to these things, and made grunting and other noises of happiness as she chomped her way through hers.

We mopped our faces and moved on.

Without saying a word, she left me at the door of the WMTC, nodding to a young man in uniform who whipped out a temporary pass for me and took me up to the fifth floor in an elevator and then led me to an office door half way along a long corridor, as if I was a new member of staff on my first day. Disconcertingly, there was even a little sign on the door with my name on it, alongside that of my officemate for the day, who turned out to be a lovely fellow from Sfax called Mourad.

"Okay, then, Gavvy," Mourad started, which incensed me the first time, although I quickly grew to like it. "Here is your seat for today. No need to turn on your PC. I will tell you all the things to do. You like the new building?"

"Em… I suppose so. I'm not sure about the long, straight corridors, though. It makes the place seem a bit too much like a hospital, don't you think?"

Mourad leaned forward, his voice hushed: "*Mental* hospital."

"Well… I'm only here for today, I think."

"That's what they said to me, too… in 1987."

"What?"

"Joke! Joke! I am only joking, no, yes."

"Good."

"Yes, yes, yes, it's a nice building, though, at least I think, and I used to have such a nice view from here across the Lake to Salève and the Alps, you know, at least until those shits over there at the World Vegetable League built their bastard new headquarters across the street, right in the way."

"That must have been a disappointing moment."

"It made me sad, Gavvy, it really did. After all we have done for them, and their vegetables, they betrayed us."

"So…"

"Instructions for you? Yes, I have them. Go down to the Jura canteen on the first floor and find Nihal. She will be wearing a big brooch on her shoulder – a big blue flower, but I do not know flowers, so do not ask me about this and which kind of flower it is. Tell Nihal you wish to inspect the interpreting booths and check the height of the seats and make sure the new cough buttons work nicely. She will give you what you need in the booth."

"Now?"

"Yes. I think."

I enjoyed a nice hot café renversé with this Nihal lady, who proudly showed me some interpreting booths adjoining the Council's main auditorium, but they were full of trainee Chinese interpreters struggling

45

with some recorded Trump footage, so Nihal took me into a cleaning cupboard instead, and stuffed a diskette into my pocket.

I got a tram down to the city centre and wandered around for a while, as I had a bit of time to kill before my flight back to Gatwick, but just as I was taking a snap of the very beautiful Orthodox church, a couple of Russians standing outside wearing shades spoke to each other and stared at me for a bit, and then one of them suddenly started sprinting in my direction, and we had a proper chase, running across roads and dodging cars and everything.

- I bet you're disappointed it wasn't filmed, aren't you?

- I hadn't thought of that. I do hope it wasn't.

So, we must have run at least half a mile, and the guy was only two or three yards behind me at a couple of points, audibly snarling. I pelted across the road into the Jardin Anglais, glancing behind me to see the guy unzipping his leather jacket as he ran, revealing his Do I Fucking *Look* Like a People Person? t-shirt. Unfortunately, in that second and a half of looking behind me I banged into the plastic lower bun of a hamburger stand designed to resemble a giant hamburger. I rolled around on the ground in agony, worried I'd snapped my pelvis or something, and I thought it would all be over in the next two seconds, if this bastard had been instructed to dispatch me straight away, but, incredibly, some fine upstanding officer of Geneva's cantonal police force was good enough to rugby-tackle the guy, which gave me enough time to jog along to the Pont du Mont-Blanc, which I then crossed.

- But did the police not come and ask you for a statement?

- Heh heh… There were only the two of them there, and they were too busy restraining the Russian. I imagine they must have sent an officer to try and find me, but I'd already moved on and had put my Leo Sayer wig in a bin. When I felt safe enough to stop, I found a nice Turkish canteen sort of place in the Pâquis, where I sat and chomped on some kebab and salad and drank some Efes and tried to forget all about it.

Ten

- Have you ever done a job in America?

- Only the once.

- How did it go? And do you remember what was on the person's t-shirt?

- You're obsessed with that!

- It's your bonkers system.

- So, I had to go to New York. I remember it for a few reasons, the top three being, one, the bagels; two, yes, the t-shirt; and three, the fact it was the only time I was given the necessary on a microfilm. It was like being in *Mission: Impossible*. Brilliant, eh!

- No doubt, Gavin.

- The bagel joint was on 6th Avenue, if I remember rightly. You ask for ham, and you think they might be generous and give you at least three slices of ham, but you haven't braced yourself for the entire fucking packet of ham wedged inside the bagel, have you, along with the pickle and the stack of Monterey fucking Jack and the fucking—

- You're getting far too emotional about this bagel, Gavin.

- Yes. Yes, I know. Sorry.

- I met the gentleman at the café. He looked vaguely uncomfortable to be there. And it was fortunate he approached slowly, as there was plenty of reading matter to take in: besides his theologically supercharged version of a red MAGA hat, namely 'Don and God Make America Great Again,' was his mauve-coloured tee with the subtly italicised legend 'Last Time I Ejaculated It Was Inside My Wife.'

The conversation went like:

"Hey, buddy," he said.

"Hi," Gavin offered.

"Huh. This?"

Gavin sort of cocked his head over to one side to acknowledge his time reading the man's proclamation. The man smiled, satisfied at Gavin's appreciation of his chest.

"Vermont. Well."

"Sorry?"

"People in Vermont. I mean everywhere, but Vermont, Jeez. They really don't know what to think when they see this. Look at you funny."

"Yeah."

"But I ain't even gonna tell you I know what they're thinking. Truth is, I don't."

"Okay. Listen… I'm wondering if you've got something for me."

"Cuttin to the chase there, buddy. Number?"

"Four thousand and five."

"You bet. And?"

"Oh yes…" I unzipped my jacket to reveal my own 'Unexpected Item in Bagging Area' t-shirt.

And he told me what to do.

You want more?

- Not especially. Nice try with going into the third person again, by the way, but I knew you couldn't keep it up.

You said it was a good 10 years before you went back to—

Eleven

- It was indeed a good 10 years before I went back to Ukraine. It was a different world. There were no more temporary coupons for a start - that was the temporary currency that they—
- Yes. I know.
- The hryvnya was declared as the new currency precisely because—
- Because the Russians have a hard time pronouncing it.
- Exactly. As the guy in that film *Kolya* says—
- "Such a great power, but they can't say the letter H."
- So, I went to Kiev, Kyiv if you will, with my friends Ian and Bert.
- "Ian and Bert." Come on!
- Like it or not, they're really fucking called Ian and Bert! And they're dear friends, too.
- Okay, okay! Why has that made you angry? It's precisely the sort of thing you should be expecting me to check.
- Apologies. They really are called Ian and Bert. But in a calmer voice. Like this. Sorry. You have every right to ask for clarifications.
- I can't help thinking your reaction here is the most convincing thing I've got out of you so far. Something about Ian and/or Bert.
- Shall I carry on?
So, we landed at Borispol, Borispil if you will, and I got in my much-needed Russian practice on the way in from the airport in the taxi. It was the best motorway I have ever seen. I painted an unfavourable portrait of the M8 to the driver by way of comparison, and he didn't believe me.
I quite liked the hotel. If you were clever, you sussed out there was a secret wee bar on the 11th floor, which was where, at the risk of product placement, I first enjoyed the most wonderful liquid that is

Chernigovskaya vodka, the drinking of which is like being socked in the face with a velvet boxing glove. I know it makes me sound like a snob, but we didn't want to get stuck at the little bar down on the ground floor and get into any trivial but potentially hazardous conversations with the crowds of punters.

- What crowds of punters?

- Roughly half the population of Bathgate, I'd say. Whereas we decided that the wee bar on the 11th floor was for the officer class, like us.

- 'Officer class'? 'Bathgate'?

- Yes. Tartan Army. I should have explained: attending the Ukraine v Scotland qualifier was part of our cover for being there.

- How fun!

- Not especially. It marked the end of a great run of results. Shevchenko was on good form, unfortunately. Walter Smith's last game in charge if I remember rightly, and the home fans on the upper tier threw cigarette packets and pastry products down onto us.

- Better than cups of piss, Gavin.

- How right you are, Leena. Actually, they were fine really, the locals. Their riot police wore big Darth Vader helmets, and we all sang the Imperial March on the way out the stadium, and the polis were all laughing away, and we were going up and shaking hands with them, and—

- Yes, yes, very Tartan Army and all that.

- Although we had some odd encounters, too. A few unsavoury hooligan types were around, offering camaraderie through xenophobia and fighting, disappointed their kilted visitors didn't want to join in… and speaking of kilts, we were challenged by one old lady at the Lavra monastery who thought we were cross-dressing and hence insulting God, at which point I started remonstrating with her and recalling our joint enterprise in 1945 and kilted Scottish soldiers greeting their Red Army comrades on the Elbe and so on, which usually sorts things out, but even that didn't get her onside.

And then there was the actual conversation I was there for, which was cunningly disguised as an incidental few words in a hotel corridor.

Do you know about *dezhurniye*, Leena?

- A *dezhurnaya* is the lady in charge of each hotel floor.

- Exactly right. So, I pass my dezhurnaya on the way to take the lift down to breakfast in the morning, and I say 'Good morning' in Ukrainian, and she says 'Good morning' back in Russian, which intrigues me. And then I ask her if it's best to hand my room key into reception when I leave the hotel for the day, or if it's okay to keep it with me, because I genuinely wasn't sure what the best thing was, or if they might be strict about it, and you always want to keep on the right side of your hosts, especially when hordes of your countrymen are sitting around the hotel sweating, drinking and talking incessantly and noisily about sweating and drinking—

- You're such a snob.

- So, I asked her about what to do with my room key, and I was absolutely gobsmacked at her reply.

- Did you get shouted at?

- Well, no – that's the amazing thing. She said *"Kak vam udobno."*

- As in, 'Whatever is most convenient for you.'

- Exactly. I just about fainted. Truly the Soviet era had faded into the past.

- And then on the second morning, the same thing happens again on the 'good morning' front: *"Dobroho ranku,"* I say; *"Dobroye utro,"* she replies, like she's correcting me again. And then I say something about how the sun will be shining for six hours, and how many men will catch big fish in the little inlet of the Dnipro next to the hotel, and she says, *"T-shirt: pokazhitye!"*

- Ha ha! And what did it say?

- If I remember, this was the 'Uglier Than You… But Sweeter!' one. It amused the dezhurnaya slightly.

"Middle drawer under television," she said.

- So… What was it? Did you go back to your room?

- I left it until after I'd come back up from my breakfast.

- So… What was it, then? Memory stick? Tape? Documents of some sort?

- Yes.

- Specifically?

- I can't tell you any more.

Pause

- Is that it? You sound like you've finished. As in, *finished*, finished.

- Yes. That's it.

I see you've taken a huge amount of notes. That's great. That's exactly what you should have done.

- How long have I got?

- Three days, I guess. Four at a push. Put your response in an A4 envelope and post it to me at the address at the bottom of your confirmation email.

- Post it?

- Yes. If you can finish it over the weekend and get it in the post on Monday, that would be the best thing. If the postmark on the envelope is any later than Tuesday, you're disqualified.

- And… Are there any instructions on format?

- Not as such. If it was me, I'd write out a summary of everything I've told you, and just put 'true' and 'false' all over it, in brackets. *Square* brackets. We like them.

- Okay.

And am I expected to include my reasoning?

- Up to you. If you think it would be useful.

- Is the aim to get as much right as possible?

- Pretty much. You've not got many rivals, but we will take a percentage count, and if you do well, then you're through to the final stage.

- Final stage?

- Well – we tell you that, but it's a lie. There's another two hoops to go through after that, I think, but the point is to be patient and persevere.

- Okay. Is that it?

- That's it.

- Can I tell you something, Gavin?

- Of course.

- Lay off both my sisters if you ever see them, for any reason.

- There's nothing I can really say about that.

- No, listen to me. This is a clear instruction, from me to you: don't fucking touch either of them. You hear?

For the first time, I clicked my pen and made a note.

The following week, I made my recommendation to the board.

THE LONGEST NIGHT

Quentin felt thirsty. He asked Ally if there was any soda left in her can, but she shook her head. It was beginning to get light: the oaks and the maple were standing out, darker than the sky again.

"What happens now?" Ally asked her brother, looking up at him. Her hair was messy, and her dungarees had gotten damp.

"Something must have happened," Quentin replied, without knowing quite why he said it.

He felt disappointed not so much because of the lack of surprises or weird events during the night; more because he had let down his sister. Mom would be pretty mad. Dad would be back home from his Denver business trip by the end of the next day, and he'd hear all about it.

Quentin felt his stomach go heavy with the realization that Mom might be awake in the house, and looking for them. What if she had seen they were missing and phoned Dad?

Leaning against the tree, Ally was still engrossed with the prospect of some sort of action taking place at any moment, although there had been a complete lack of it, and time was nearly up. At 3.30 in the morning she had cried and hugged Quentin because she had gotten scared, but he was brave, and the wind that had chilled her hadn't lasted too long.

"It's five thirty," she stated, having pushed the little button on her Lisa Simpson watch that made the light come on.

"I figure we should maybe go inside now," suggested Quentin. He was nine.

"It's not quite light yet," she said. "That means it's not day."

"I guess." Quentin wasn't going to argue. He had seen nothing. He now firmly believed that the night-time was kind of overrated, and that they shouldn't repeat the experience. Their heads were both spinning in a way that neither of them recognized. Even if the stuff he had heard in the playground had been contradictory, it had seemed worth investigating. What did Ally believe? The same, he guessed.

"We should maybe wait another half an hour. Then it'll actually be light and night'll be over."

"Okay," said Quentin, feeling deeply tired and wondering what in the world his little sister must think of him. He hadn't *promised* her that something would happen, but she must have gotten the impression from the way he had talked to her that he really believed there would be something to see, something that was always going on out there in the dark, maybe every night, shielded from them in their sleep. So said the playground.

Ally was only six.

With the slowly spreading light, there was more and more to look at, and the two blond, mussed-up heads did some more scrutinizing of the yard, the trees, the garage and all around.

There was no noise. The RV was easy to pick out now, sitting on the drive, all its surfaces covered in big drips left over from the shower (and thank goodness it had only been a brief shower).

Only ten more minutes went by before Ally suggested it really was time to go indoors. Quentin wasn't going to argue. He watched his sister rub her eyes and yawn.

Yesterday, as part of the planning, they had talked several times about stepping across the porch and closing the doors real quiet, so they did that, without any need to remind each other. They padded up the carpeted stairs.

They passed the door to the rumpus room, then Mom and Dad's room. There was a light showing underneath the door.

Quentin carried on walking to his bedroom. Ally stayed still. They waved to each other. Quentin went to his bed, leaving the door half open. Ally felt her hair: it was a little wet. She went to the bathroom, had a pee and washed her hands. Then she used the white towel to dry her hair as much as she could.

Mom had put her PJs under her top pillow, as usual, and Ally put them on quickly. She wondered if Mom was awake. And her tummy was sore all of a sudden. She needed to tell Mom.

She slowly opened the door to her parents' bedroom.

"Mom?"

Her 34-year-old mother was sitting up in bed, only her crossed legs covered by the sheets. She had nothing on, and there were goose bumps all over her breasts and shoulders. Four big red candles that Ally had never seen before were standing on the dresser, all burning. A picture of a man was up on the wall. It looked like Dad, wearing something like a big, white bathrobe. But Ally wasn't really sure.

Mom was staring, just staring at the picture. And she was making a murmuring noise and her lips were moving.

"Mom."

She didn't answer.

"Mom, can you hear me?"

Ally went into Quentin's room. He had left the bedside light on. He must have fallen asleep real fast.

"Quentin." His eyebrows twitched. "Quentin, wake up. Quent."

He murmured. He moved his head from side to side. "Ally?" he said.

"Quentin."

"What time is it now?"

"Just after six o'clock."

"Are you okay? What's up?"

"I saw it."

"What?" Quentin sat up and rubbed his face. His sister looked deadly serious. "Well, what was it? Have you been back outside?"

"No." Ally looked down at the floor for a few seconds and stared blankly. Then she looked back into the eyes of her brother.

"It was here in the house all the time."

The Birks, 2021

The cowrin couple up the corner
Gie the Persian man their order
(Altho we're miles fae Persia's border):
Kebabs of Aberfeldy.

He taks the orders, washes, dries.
"He's versatile!" the gillie cries.
Our dining pleasure lights his eyes:
Kebabs of Aberfeldy.

Noo it's oor turn tae command
A dish or twa fae that far land:
An ashet piled wi salad and
Kebabs of Aberfeldy.

A chiel maun niver eat bad chicken,
Undercooked. You'll surely sicken
Unless a spicy sauce they thicken
In a kitchen
(In Aberfeldy).

"It's ben the fire," oor host assures
That's gey guid news: nae scran ae oors
Will poison us, and nor will yours:
Kebabs of Aberfeldy

Rice and meze… sic a dinner!
Every dish a sure-fire winner
Gin they're chicken, mixed or doner
Kebabs of Aberfeldy
The End.

MRS FIGGIT'S FOUR HUNDRED AND SIXTY-SEVENTH CUP OF TEA

Well, honestly, I'm thinking. She really ought to be here by now.

I finished the pork for lunch – together with the cabbage, even though it was getting somewhat elderly – and the washing up is all done. It's well past a quarter to two – well, there's the two o'clock news bulletin on the wireless, in fact. Perhaps I shall go and listen to it.

She said a quarter to two on the telephone. That was her promise. Her usual time.

Is she well? Could she have died since her ten o'clock telephone call? I clasp my hands together in thought. I look in the bureau for my pocket calculator. I depress the orange plastic keys as I think, and watch the green electronic lights tell me the answer: if one person dies every two seconds – goodness knows where I get that idea from (the television no doubt) – Mrs Figgit would be in the company of more than seven thousand souls since ten o'clock.

I muse, and then think nothing of it. I can't seem to visualise seven thousand dead people, although I find it a great deal easier – a *great* deal easier – to visualise a dead Mrs Figgit on her own.

A dead Evelyn Figgit would be an unmitigated disaster. Softly cranky and dreadfully irritating she might be, but she would make me very upset were she to turn out to be dead this lunchtime.

I tremble with the thought, and decide to listen to what they're saying on the wireless.

"Honestly," I say to myself in my nice, fruity, ridiculous voice, "they really should let that nice old Chilean senator go home now. Tut!"

I spotted a stain on my bedroom curtains earlier this morning, so I proceed through, my paranoia at Figgit's tardiness receding to mere annoyance. There it is. Yellowish. Can't go getting the stain remover out now, though, as I'd have to put on my gloves, and what if Mrs Figgit turns up just as I make a start? She only would.

I think of the second bottom drawer of my bedside cabinet. Do you know what I keep in there? Two sets of darts. I choose the set that my old friend Claudia gave me.

I glance through the hallway to the front door. Still no sign. I mince over to the dressing table and reverse the mirror on its hinge. On the back, framed by green baize cloth, is a dartboard. On the dartboard is a colour photograph cut out from a newspaper, centred perfectly.

I can't decide whether to remove the picture and play proper darts or to improve my aim on the Prime Minister's smugly grinning and make-up-caked face.

I decide. The first shot lands one sixteenth of an inch above his right eye. Wonderful! The second hits a nondescript place just above the hairline. The third... does not get a chance to be thrown. At last, the doorbell! I retrieve the darts – one is tough to get out, and I'm afraid I emit a bit of a grunt retrieving it – and return the mirror to its habitual aspect.

"Coming, Evelyn," I cry as I approach the front door – it can't be anyone else.

And there she is. I know that the afternoon will proceed just the same as usual: farting, cups of tea and chat. Not in that order – one never needs pay attention to the order of such things. One is the reason, the other is the focal point and the third is a mishap of life as a mammal.

Coffee used to be my thing, but I must confess my discontinuation is a matter of necessity, not of a change in taste. I certainly can't take all the espresso I once used to – given my bowels, you see. Miss it terribly, though.

Now, I shall not present a verbatim transcript of the conversation I have with Mrs F at the front door, you have to allow me that.

Although it is an idea, I suppose. If I did, it would probably start off something like:

Figgit: Ooh. Hello, dear.
Semple: Hello, Evelyn, in you come, dear.
Figgit: Ah.
Semple: Mmm hmm.
Figgit: Right.
Semple: Put a kettle on. Mmm?
Figgit: Hmm. Ah.
Semple: Your coat, hmm?

Figgit: There we –
Semple: Mmm hmm. There we –
Figgit: Right.

And so on.

I much prefer the

"Hello dear," says Mrs Figgit as I open the door.

"In you come, Evelyn," I say, noticing the same ink stain on her blouse as last time – and therefore noting that it is the same blouse. "I'll just put the kettle on, shall, I?"

Evelyn smiles and I gesture for her to take her coat off (surprising with this weather, really) so that I can pop it on the spare room bed before I go off to the kitchen. "There we are," I say, leaving her to go through and lower herself into a sitting room chair, as I fill up the kettle with water – knowing what a frightful temper could be aroused were I to try and help her into her seat.

Better.

Not untypically, and to my not inconsiderable annoyance, Mrs Figgit starts to talk about almost everything under the sun *while I'm through making the tea.* In other words, her remarks are entirely *inaudible* to me. She is in the sitting room; I am in the kitchen, and so I CANNOT HEAR HER. In a much-practised move, I fetch the carton of full-fat milk and plonk it down heavily on the sideboard, fish some teaspoons out of the drawer and shower all two of them down as well, already leading off with my left foot and perambulating myself to the sitting room. Within three feet of the door, in my fruity yet sharp voice that I always use to Mrs Figgit and other contemporaries when addressing them in the middle distance, I call out, "Tea first, Mrs Figgit, now you really *must* have some tea in front of you before you go telling me about all your doings and your news, hmm?" I detect uncertainty in the second or two of silence that follow, so I add, "I can't hear you if I'm through in the kitchen, now, hmm?"

Mrs Figgit, says, "Righto, dear," in a pathetic, hurt sort of way, which I find quite wretched, I really do. She has no tough exterior, that one, yet she gives every impression of believing that hers is 'an exalted and central seat in the cosmos', to use one of my dear late mother's expressions. In other words, she is affronted every time the world does not allow her to do just as she pleases. For instance, the laws of physics insult her when she cannot make herself heard muttering to the receptionist in the clinic DESPITE THE FACT THERE IS A FIRE ALARM; the laws of the road hurt her feelings when she steps in front of a moving vehicle during the red man and she is tooted at; she is cruelly neglected when her cleaning lady cannot come on Tuesday through a broken arm; and it is inexplicable that she can have been passed over for consultation when the tennis starts early and she can't listen to 'Antiques this Forenoon' on the television at the proper time. Every single accident of circumstance, happenstance, coincidence or wild nature is unacceptable if it is taken without consulting Mrs Figgit first, and that entire slew of injustice is conveyed to me by her RIGHTO and its tone.

But I will *not* run into the hall every fifteen seconds to listen to her remarks, scuttle back to the kitchen to pop in one teabag while shouting my reply at the top of my voice only then to sprint back again for her rejoinder. I am in control.

But most of all, I am relieved she is here. At how disastrous it would have been had she never turned up I have already hinted, I know. And her lateness is not uncommon.

Oh, you mustn't even think about asking yourself *why* Mrs Figgit is late. That is not, how shall I put it, at stake. When her *Herald* is late, then there's a fuss, and she has a watch on her wrist all of a sudden, oh yes. Not that she can read anything smaller than the headlines, I shouldn't wonder. But her coming here? Late? On time? Arrangements? Who do I think I am? She comes. She comes at a certain time, measurable by watch, cuckoo clock, oven timer and all, but that time of day is not important, is it? I don't have other things to do, do I? Good Lord, the last time I popped out for a walk round the garden when she was already nearly an hour late, she made a frightful fuss, hopping up and down on the doorstep like a sparrow in the wrong tree, darting her eyes about at all sorts of ridiculous angles.

Back through in the kitchen, I cock my head to one side to listen carefully for a second or two, making sure Figgit has not got up from her seat in the living room for some reason. I open the cupboard door. Behind the ironing board is a blackboard, on which is written the number four hundred and sixty-six, circled. I write 467, and will circle it and erase the 466 after the cup of tea – that cup of tea now on my small little pine tray – has been consumed and has disappeared down the gullet (what a thought!) of Evelyn Figgit.

My chalking-up of what I call the tea index figure – I am now into my bigger packet of chalk, which is yellow – is something of an automatic routine, and today is one of those few occasions when I actually give it some thought. I will never forget the three hundred and tenth, which ended up with my scalding poor Figgit's front when some daft old bat crashed her Morris straight into the back of an Allander's bus just outside the house. It was a dreadful thing. The elderly Mrs Shriever in question cannot now speak at all apart from making a noise like 'beeeeeee' and, poor thing, is no longer driving.

All the other times were as forgettable as I expect this one to be – they are nothing in my memory. I cannot even picture the Figgit (or the me!) of six years ago, when the Tea Programme was still a young process and, frankly, it doesn't matter.

The tea: I put it in front of her, and the plate of bloody miserable shortbread, and remind her, "Probably still a little too hot dear, shall we leave it a minute or two, hmm?"

She looks at me with a vacant yet unnervingly hurt look, as if I've just told her I'll have to confiscate all her property.

"Did you see the weather?" asks Evelyn, in exactly the tone of voice that one would use when asking "Did you hear the news about that homosexual on the wireless?" I am a bit taken aback, and struggle to make sense of what she means by '*the weather*'.

"You mean the wind and showers last night?"

"Kept awake all night," she reports, with her trademark skeletal use of English syntax. "Heard a fox, and I heard the mail plane, and I heard cars. There were people. Talking. One was a woman."

"Oh, really! Some people will come and go at the oddest of hour, Evelyn, dear – they just do."

"Well not this one, Doreen, no, it was a car."

"Well…" I struggle.

"They were talking so loudly. I thought they might be coming up to my door, so I made sure my light was off."

"Yes, well, I…"

"I used to sleep so soundly, Doreen, dear," continues Figgit, and already the muscles in my head are contorted with semi-suppressed urges to yawn. "But now I…"

A pause. Nothing. Yes?

DON'T ANY MORE, I scream at her mentally. FINISH YOUR BLOODY SENTENCES!

She shakes or, more accurately, wobbles her head from side to side.

Figgit, with no intention of completing her grammatical duty to the language, then stares at me as if my thoughts are audible. Or she may be looking quizzical because I've farted. Have I? It's quite possible.

It is moments like these when I thank my lucky stars I haven't kept a pistol under my seat cushions – or a throwing knife – because God only knows I've proved wonderfully dextrous using both weapons in the arena of my imagination.

Like an excited lover, however, I realise that a golden opportunity is in front of me to steer the conversation. The excitement comes not of passion, though, but merely out of the thrilling prospect of avoiding the lowest level of spirit-smashing boredom that comes if one listens to Evelyn Figgit's unchecked prattling for too long.

"And is your eldest well?"

"Malcolm? He's back in Ardrossan this week."

I have just penned the line containing the word 'Ardrossan'. Now, that might not seem awfully noteworthy, unless, perhaps, you do not know this corner of this island and, locating Ardrossan in a world atlas, imagine it to be some sort of Coney Island. The fact that Figgit has said "He's [...] in Ardrossan" is one of the most shatteringly tremendous things that has happened in my long, uneventful and frankly tortuous relationship with Evelyn Doris Figgit.

You do not yet understand the nuances of the situation, but you may be astute enough to deduce that Evelyn Figgit, in all my tea-soaked conversations with her to date, three quarters of which have at least mentioned the existence of her 37-year-old son, Malcolm, has only just now mentioned his geographical whereabouts for the first time ever.

I cannot tell you how much time I've spent wondering where that boy was. I had imagined central London, of course, or possibly Cheltenham or, for some reason, Fife. If not, then somewhere around the Moray Firth, the Outer Hebrides, west Wales, Cambridgeshire or Swindon. But not even in my darkest dreams did the Ayrshire coast come into my thinking.

I don't know Ardrossan at all. I know the train goes there from Central, I can roughly visualise its location on a map, and I imagine one must be able to see Arran from it, and now I think about it, I'm pretty sure that's where the ferry goes from – so I must have passed through the town as a child. But I can barely picture the place, other than to wonder if it's anything like Largs, which I suspect it isn't.

But now I have to say something in reaction, something that will get me more.

"Is he enjoying it there at the moment?"

My heart sinks as the chain of conversation already seems to have found a rotten link. Figgit gives me a look that says, "Oh. I've just said 'Ardrossan' in front of you."

"I'm not supposed to tell you," states Evelyn.

Keeping my lady's smile, I just say, "Oh, do they not like you talking to other people about it, then?"

"No, not really," she replies. Ah, good: at least I now know that there really is a *they*. "They don't let me talk to him very much at all, sometimes. You know I only see him every month or six weeks now, Doreen, dear."

"Oh dear, yes, I know. Drink up some of your tea, now."

Her sagging lower lip curls irregularly round the edge of the bone china and she tilts the cup until hot tea trickles away into her mouth.

"And what is it they make him do to work such long hours? He does work long hours, doesn't he?"

Forlorn, Figgit nods. "Secret. I mustn't tell you. Bombs."

I struggle to control myself. A lapse into profound catatonic shock would be perfectly appropriate at this point; or I could goggle at Figgit with transfixed rigidity, my mouth gaping open, suppressing my hysterical screams just enough to reduce them to pitiful high-pitched whimpers; a further option would be to pounce over, grab her by the lapels of her somewhat tired tweed blazer and bark out a series of questions.

No, no. I do not want her to tighten her wobbling and loose lips at the moment, and I judge that it would be best to carry on up the gentle, leafy gradient of Subtle Avenue, with my questions placed like quiet, well interspersed bus stops, not like tightly packed, conspicuous gaggles of agitated, hopping pedestrians.

"Oh what a business it must be, Evelyn, with those bombs." I sip some more tea, aching with longing that it were in fact gin, as Evelyn nods uncertainly.

"I would hate to have to work with bombs," I put in a few seconds later, instantly worried I'm pushing too much and too quickly. Her reaction to this remark is not entirely calm, but nor is it unpromising. She turns her pallid face to me and frowns in an extraordinarily gradual way. She says, "It's not really the bombs."

My stomach sinks. I fear I might have to start again.

"He works... well, it's what you call monitoring, I think. They decide what to do if there are bombs coming."

My mind races. This is extraordinary. "Oh," I say, "for emergencies, then?"

Having already turned towards me, she cocks her head to a diagonal angle in order to express her surprise: "Yes. Do you know about it too?"

In all the godawful, creakingly slow, repetitive, mind-numbing, here-we-go-again, tea-centred, fart-punctuated, asinine, foolish, pointless, fruitless and generally unsatisfactory six hundred and umpety-ump conversations that I have had with this dreadful old woman, I have never had to think so hard as in the last minute or so. I can even feel the sweat on my brow.

"And all the evacuation plans," says Figgit, popping her words out in telegraphic non-sentences that I simply cannot afford to misinterpret.

Taking hold of my teacup again, I look up to check that she isn't going to attach a predicate to her most recent words. No. So I am left with 'the evacuation plans'. This is rather difficult. No sooner, however, does it occur to me to pray to the Almighty for inspiration than she says something else.

"Malcolm says that if Scotland ever goes its own way, they have that place to sort of, you know, spy and keep an eye on things. There's a hotline to Whitehall, or something. It's very… he mustn't tell me about it and when he said… you know, hush-hush… he said he shouldn't have… I mean, I oughtn't tell anyone…"

I sip the last bit of my first cup of tea loudly, and try to stop her getting there. "Must be quite a place, then," I say. "Underground I expect."

"Oh yes. It's in the basement of a café where they serve ice cream and, you know… *burgers*."

I nod slowly, my head popping violently in a million colours on the inside. And then she catches up with herself.

"Oh, Doreen, I mustn't tell you, you know."

"Oh, don't worry, Evelyn, I won't…"

"I mustn't tell anybody."

"Now, don't worry at all, Evelyn."

"I shouldn't have said anything about…"

"No, no, Evelyn, you just, um… I haven't heard anything of what you've just said, now, have I?"

"But," she says hollowly, her veins looking blue and troubled, "I just told you about that café by the seafront…"

At this point I am quite ready to break into nervous giggles, and I have to put a hand over my mouth. I adjust my position on the seat and, just as I am wondering whether to cough, I find myself taken without warning by the outrush of a steady and headstrong fart. I have broken wind in front of Evelyn Figgit well over a thousand times over the years, but that doesn't make it any less, how should I put it, *irreconcilable*.

"Oh, I…" I start, and fish about my hip for a handkerchief, but not having pockets today realise it's up my right sleeve. I blow my nose and screech as I am doing so to avoid laughing too obviously. Figgit, in her typical reaction, grabs for her cup of tea, and takes at least half the cup at once, already eyeing the pot for the obligatory fill-up.

"Now…"

"Oh, Doreen," Evelyn says, putting her hands on the edge of the tray, "I really oughtn't to have told you about Malcolm's work."

"My lips are sealed."

"It's terribly secret."

"It's not my business anyway, Evelyn. It's just nice to hear that Malcolm's doing well, dear, that's all."

"It's *terribly* secret."

"Now have some more tea."

"I should be doing some of my shopping. I need eggs and some rolls for the morning. And milk, I'm sure."

"Well, now, Evelyn," I say. She takes the teapot and pours tea almost to the brim of her cup, her hand far too loose on the handle. It hardly leaves any for me, in fact. Not that I give two hoots, of course. Anyway, she drinks it reasonably quickly, sucking her lips between sips, not spilling any. She had been gazing aimlessly into the middle distance for most of the conversation; now she is looking so intently at the pink-painted radiator in the corner that I worry it may burst.

I have asked; she has spoken – now the minutes seem to last forever. She generates one of her trademark peep-type farts as she gets up for her ritual nose powdering before leaving to go back to her own house, on Campsie Drive.

As she is through in the bathroom making an assortment of coughing, gentle retching and anal sounds, I think of punching the air like they do a lot on the television, but instead I just think, examine my fingernails and briefly cover my face with my hands.

To my wantonly intense pleasure, when Evelyn comes out of the bathroom she does that pathetic, aimless sort of dance she always does, which indicates to me that she would now like to collect her coat and leave.

"I'll just get your coat, now, shall I, hmm?" It's a bit like the start, but in reverse. Assuring her that she has her brolly, I see her off my threshold. She gives her usual awkward little wave and heads along the pavement, wobbling carelessly despite the myriad times she has negotiated the particular irregularities in the tarmacadam immediately beyond the gate in my hedge.

"Cheerio," I say.

As soon as I am in the kitchen, I reach for the Glenmorangie and pour myself a big one. I think for a second about how short a time it might be before I have to get into the car, decide bugger it, and sink it. I check my watch, then go through to the front room to take a look out the curtains, just to make sure Figgit has rounded the corner.

Clear.

I'm in such a fluster I wonder what to do first. Realising the implications, and getting a rush on the thrill of release, I go to the bathroom to remove my lipstick and makeup. I get changed far less methodically than usual, dumping my stockings on the floor and shoving the skirt in the drawer without folding it. I enjoy a few seconds of scratching around the general area of my underpants and kneel down besides the bed so that I can get at the silver briefcase underneath it. I pull it out and look at my watch again. Five past three.

Having drawn the curtains closed, I place the briefcase on one of my silly little tables and pull out the two antennae to their maximum extent. I punch in my code and take the wig off as I'm waiting.

"G."

"G? It's A. I've done it." My voice is almost trembling.

"Archie? You really?"

"The nest, and some sort of monitoring centre for bomb strikes it seems. Bit out of date, potentially, but still operational. Falls into place as part of the network, I think."

"Wow!" G seems really pleased.

"Surface location is here in Scotland. It's a café selling fast food, ice cream and so on, near foreshore, Ardrossan, Ayrshire. You got that?"

There is a pause. "Right, terrific, you can leave the ground-work to us. We'll give you a full debriefing tomorrow night at Base One."

"Tomorrow? Okay… And a new assignment?"

"I should very much think so, Archie."

"I'll need a ticket to Havana, then."

"Of course. I'll make sure one of the guys meets you at Heathrow for a mini-brief this evening, so get yourself down there. We'll sort the rest out."

I sign off, re-scramble the frequency settings and shove the antennae back in. I'll have to contact Dan the Undertaker Man sooner rather than later, but I can sort that out over the phone while I'm waiting at Glasgow Airport. Time to get moving.

I don't take long in the shower. I finish drying my hair and throw the towel onto the discarded stockings. The doors and windows are all locked, the alarm is timed to activate in ten minutes and my bag is zipped closed.

I depress the green knob and sit wistfully as I glide downward with ludicrous slowness on the stairlift, which had been intended, as I recounted more than once to Evelyn Figgit, for the use of my older sister so that she could move in and stay with me – although that never transpired in the end, of course, because she was bumped off by that awful burglar from Drumchapel.

The bottom four steps retract, and I sink down under the floor of the house. Eventually I am tipped forward and the familiar leather of my Lotus greets my bottom. The underside of the staircase seals up again and the green communicator light on the dashboard winks on as the soft top folds itself over my head. I adjust my tie and scan the receiver to see if I have any priority messages. Just the one: "British Airways 17:55 shuttle – usual account". Efficient of them.

The runners under the vehicle finish their track; daylight spills onto the top of the car. The rectangle opens up, widens and becomes square. Little clods of soil and a few scraps of chrysanthemum – this part always irritates me – plop onto the bottom of the windscreen, scattering themselves below the wipers so they'll be annoying me all journey. Balls!

Finally, though, the hydraulics lift me up onto nextdoor's driveway.

There's a bit of a long wait at the Cross, and when I get to Canniesburn Toll some moron signals left but swings round right in front of me, making me do an emergency stop. Milngavie wanker. I give him the Vs too late.

Seven years. Seven fucking years. My funeral was going to be an absolute pleasure.

"Thanks so much for coming, thank you very much… Ah, hello, Evelyn."

"Oh, Archibald. So sorry."

"I know how much Doreen depended on your visits, Evelyn."

"I must have known her for oh, the last seven years. Or eight, perhaps."

"Yes, Evelyn, I'm sure it must have been about that long."

"You look so alike."

"Yes, a lot of people say that. And she was such a big girl of course – I was barely taller than her."

"You'll come and see me… I don't know."

"Yes, I've…"

"You've got her house now."

"Ah… Yes… How did…?"

"You're moving back through here from Edinburgh, you'll still work for your management consultancy from home and you've got your sister's house now. That's good. You were back so late last night. I couldn't sleep. Was that your car, the Lotus?"

I am sliding from confused, via perplexed and disturbed, to horrified.

I look up. For a second or two I notice nothing apart from the edges of the white clouds, where water droplets have ruffled themselves into a cotton rampart against the hard blue. All sorts of twittie-birds sing, reminding me of the lush trees around us.

"But you're round the other side of the hill, Evelyn, so how on earth do you kn…?"

"You're about to get important information on the change in the Moscow situation," announces Figgit, which causes the whole world to shimmer in front of me. "I think you might find, Archie, that we're effectively on the same team from now on," she says in a solid tone quite new to me, straightening herself up to a previously unadvertised height. "Perhaps you should come round to mine for your cup of tea tomorrow, for a change."

ENID

Enid rounded the corner, impressively in control, her faded cherry dress flapping audibly as the taxi swerved out into the middle of Humbert Drive to avoid her. She dealt the cabbie a piercing look of indignation.

She put the Raleigh on its stand, breathing quite heavily. "Bet you didn't find any," she challenged. Sure enough. She had a trophy to lift out of her basket and brandish in my direction: a heavy bag of red onions. And there I was, just lolling empty-handed on the doorstep.

The jingling knot of metal passed by me, tumbling, flexing through the air before I could react. "Come on," she said. I stooped to pick up the keys, feeling a bit lost. Why did she always throw things at me like that? Always testing me. The last time I'd come back with her from the market, during the Easter holidays, she had lobbed a whole pineapple through the doorway into the kitchen without any warning; it had flown right in front of my face and stunned the dog. I was starting to see what Mum meant now.

aphorisms and musings

in alphabetical order

*with greetings and respect to all those descended
from the copious children of*

François, duc de La Rochefoucauld
(1613-1680)

*and belated **hommage** to other worthy producers of
Notes and **Pensées** etcetera,
por ejemplo **Bryan Magee**, who wrote about solipsism and art and so on,
and that **Blaise Pascal**, who wrote about
the human condition and God and stuff*

*The author asserts that his musings are original and that any
duplication here of any previously uttered, published or merely mused
musings is entirely coincidental and innocent.*

(i)

1. A bag that has the sauce that was meant to be on your kebab last
night smeared all over the inside of it is not the bag that you should take
along to that finance steering committee meeting tomorrow.

2. A book, it is said, can take you anywhere. How exhilarated we feel, though, when that place is just down the road.

2B: A dirtier, cheesier, creamier British-Italian carbonara I've never had. Thank you, as ever, Aberfeldy.
[*for The Consequence, see 172B*]

3. A nice fresh bagel will improve almost every conceivable situation.

4. A shadow tastes of nothing.

5. A true coward is the man who will not remove a tea bag with his fingers.

6. Although in Edinburgh you can signal a bus to stop with one eyebrow, this is not usually enough in Glasgow.

7. An argument is best won when both sides of it are acknowledged as valid, preferably in a courteous manner. Unless, of course, the other side is self-evidently a big heap of pish.

8. Analytical people like journeys; sensual people like travel; only well-balanced, broad-minded freaks like both.

9. Any apparent male complexities are in fact mostly a result of sheer thoughtlessness. If men actually worked at being complicated, it would all fall apart very quickly.

10. Any decent history of Scotland will record that, amid the flurry of excitement about expanding communications technology and dotcom companies at the dawn of the 21st century, the milk carton took on an impressive new role in keeping the populace abreast of important religious and secular holidays.

11. Any German sausage except that white one, please.

12. Any type of antisocial behaviour stems from exclusion from society, whether that exclusion is actual or perceived.

13. Appreciation is not a prerequisite for gratitude.

14. Are you meant to eat the garnish?

15. Are you worried about the Yellow Peril? You needn't be. Try, instead, the nagging possibility that you left the freezer door open before you set off for the airport.

16. As war stokes terror, and terror provokes war, the decision to conduct a "war on terror" is to promote both in their cycle of violence, and to reject in perpetuity the efforts of both the Saviour and the Prophet – and many others – to teach peace. Not in my name.

17. Ask people what's inside their mouth, and it's amazing how rarely they say nitrogen.

18. At home, things make routine, comforting noises during the day and go 'bump' in the night; in foreign countries, things go 'bang' during the day and 'pip pip boooip boing eep eep aaaaaa pip crackle BANG BANG BANG BANG' during the night.

19. Attempting to make spaghetti carbonara by guessing the recipe simply will not produce a good meal.

20. Be sensitive to the feelings of the person whom you are about to correct for using an apostrophe in the wrong place. He might be a lot bigger, stronger and angrier than you.

21. [*withdrawn: my excoriating criticism of old people buying one stamp at a time in the post office was unfair and insensitive*]

22. Being meek? Face it, it's a cracking deal at the end of the day.

23. Confident people are just secretly insecure people on a roll.

24. Death unburdens even the untroubled.

25. Democracy is the mitigation of corruption through a limited degree of accountability.

26. Differences between siblings are best demonstrated through their respective appreciation for the arts.

27. Do not pass your place of work on a bicycle on a day when you have pulled a sickie.

28. Drop-chinned student sitting opposite, or rather diagonally opposite, table next to me. Okay, not student. Recent graduate. Now a few years into some comfortable corporate job. Might be about 27. Scottish middle class using American English for no fucking reason, like when the waitress asks him "Have you decided what you'd like, or do you need some more time?" he says "Yeah, I'm good."

Aarggh!

And then wittering on about going to Japan and his fucking scuba diving course, and how...

And then later it's "Would you like any other sauces with that?"

"No, I'm great, thanks."

AAAAAAAARRRRGH!

29. Dystopian fiction is not just a warning of how awful the world could be; it is also a reminder of how awful the world already is.

30. Each baby comes out of a moment.

31. Everyday life is so fucking galling.

32. Exactly half way between promise and lie, there you will find fudge.

33. Forgetting is in itself entirely forgivable, but failure to remember is not.

34. Fresh fruit, like atmospheric pollution and the emotion of love, can transcend national boundaries. A most pertinent example of this was in May 2000, when Israeli troops made a hasty withdrawal from south Lebanon. Just before the Hezbollah forces pitched up, a crowd of Lebanese Christians and others were milling about next to the border fence, looking through at the journalists and the other bods on the Israeli side. At some point, in an apparent gesture of helpfulness, one of the people on the north side lobbed a whole melon over the fence. This was, by all accounts, appreciated, as those on the south side had come with little to eat, and I venture to assume that whatever breach of excise laws may have taken place in the projection of the gourd was disregarded by the extant authorities on both sides.

35. From childhood onwards, we all measure our lives by our dental appointments and the intervals in between.

36. Getting out of bed in the morning just means going through all that fucking hassle.

37. Have you ever asked yourself what it is that makes the cod wake up at night?

38. Helping wheelchair-using Buddhist monks onto trains – time and again, it feels like the right thing to do.

39. How can a whole field be burnished? Because of the whole sky above it.

40. I Can't Believe it's not Butter. When I first heard about it, many years ago now, I reckoned such a singular American stupidity would never be sold in the UK. I was wrong.
As an old friend called Richard once postulated, the range could perhaps be extended with, for instance,
Surely These Must be Beans.
And thus:
What In Heaven's Name Is This If It's Not Guacamole?
Don't You Dare Tell My Friend These Are Not Apricots.
If You're Saying This Is Not Truly Grape Juice You Must Be A Lying Rat.
This Is Not Actually Horseradish? Stand Clear While I Punch Myself In The Face.

41. I firmly support the moral majority's view that flatulence should be suppressed in company and should not generally be spoken about. That self-conscious suppression is, however, a typification of the hypocritical standards of behaviour that prevail on this island, quite apart from being a good example of British distaste for all or any bodily function. What I'm driving at is that people can sometimes get away with being inconsiderate, rude or even violent to one another more readily than they get away with farting in each other's company.

42. I know someone who speaks to God. That's the same God who had those tricky conversations with Abraham several millennia ago; who, according to some sources, begat a famous Son who was at the same time Himself, some two thousand years ago; and/or who conveyed further powerful messages through his last Prophet a few centuries after that. Anyway, the point is that I know someone who *speaks to* this very same God. Now you must admit, that's pretty fucking impressive.

43. I live among a generation of Cureheads.

44. I once imagined I might start off my writing career with the screenplay for a vegetarian psycho-horror, but friends advised me I could never pull it off.

45. I want to find my bar of Dove free of your pubes.

46. I was delighted when Father, never usually one to address inanimate objects, cried out on Christmas day: "Sausages! You're going in next! Buggers!"

47. If a translator does more than choose the right words, it is to re-choose words that are right.

48. If a work colleague returns from a day's absence, be wary about asking him what was wrong – he might have got his tongue stuck in the icebox or done something else embarrassing that he will not want to talk about.

49. If the citizens of Edinburgh could do one little thing to make me happier, it would be to stop being quite so anal about the precise order in which one boards a bus.

50. If there is poverty, both politics and economics have failed.

50B: If you're looking for a good spoon cheese, you can't get much better than those tasty smoked applewood products you get a lot just now. You should deploy at room temperature, and it'll wash off the spoon much easier than you expect.

51. If you can persuade two Norwegian girls to come to bed with you, you must be doing something right.

52. If you have a Golden Rule for yourself in life, it's most likely about never doing that total arse-up of a thing you once did a second time.

52B. If you have grown up in a city, or suburbia, you will forever be spooked by animal viscera.

53. If you pull a jumper over your head very slowly, you momentarily find yourself in your bed again and, by extension, back in the womb.

54. If you still don't like olives, you have essentially remained a child.

55. If you wish to keep your girlfriend, do not repeatedly and loudly address her with the words "Hey, hey, Pickles!" in the supermarket.

56. If your craving to eat a white pudding supper persists beyond two-thirds of the time that it takes you to eat it, then you should have had a bigger lunch.

57. If your friend has just arrived after a long journey, treat her with compassion.

58. I'm nice sometimes.
I'm not actually very nice sometimes.

59. In a few days, it will be 2011. It really is high time for car manufacturers to stop putting in indicator lights, as their existence can occasionally give some people the impression (quaint, I know) that they are still meant to be used, for example at roundabouts or other junctions. When the law changed about this, I somehow didn't notice.

And by the way, if you're one of those people who doesn't bother signalling when you're meant to, whether it's because it's too much effort for you, or because you are simply too important to do such a banal little thing, please take the hint. Otherwise, there is a small but real chance that I will actually come along and find you and smash your arrogant fat face into a pulp. Perhaps, if you want to be confident of avoiding this, you might send me some cheques, and I can get some more psychotherapy in an attempt to calm down about this sort of stuff.

And - oh hell - I suppose I should admit that I don't use my indicators all the time myself. But only when there's definitely no-one about or when I innocently forget or am distracted by something, okay?

60. In Carntyne, you will not find all the houses.

61. In party politics, nothing is more sickening than the tendency to find every opportunity to disagree instead of seeking every opportunity to cooperate.

THE ULTIMATE MONOLOGUE
OF ANDREW MACFADYEN

"I love being surrounded by the water, so I do," proclaimed Uncle Andy. He was sitting there on the tatty wooden chair he liked so much, in his favourite spot of all, playing the boring old sea-dog. Although he easily qualified for the boring part, he had only spent two years at sea. The best years of his life, as we had heard at least a thousand times.

The lake was behind him – it was also to his left and to his right. In front of him, the jetty led back to the bottom of the lawn. The garden was ours; the water belonged to Lake George. It was spring 2002 – now some 12 years in the past. I wasn't quite a teenager yet.

"Nice here, but not the same as the sea, of course. You ever been on the ocean, Amy?"

"Sure: the Alaskan cruise last summer," I repeated for about the tenth time that week.

"Ah, fantastic country, Alaska," he breathed, only just audibly. I wondered how mad he'd get if I pointed out Alaska isn't a country but a state. Probably about as mad as that time when Jeff Hollins from the steamboat ticket office had commented that Scotland was easily his favourite part of England. I'd thought Uncle Andy was going to lose an eye that time, he turned so red.

"I've never told you how upset I was the day I heard about that Russian submarine, have I?"

Like twice is only two away from never, so I guess he was almost right.

"The St Andrew's cross it is they fly from their vessels. And when I saw that flag at half mast atop that other submarine in dock, wherever it was…" He paused as if a great revelation was squeezing through some big valve in his head.

The number of times I'd imagined the old wood of the jetty crumbling away, Andy tumbling into the water in his chair.

"Kursk!" he finally exclaimed. "The Kursk. That's the name of it. All those men."

His eyes watered. "No one so loyal. No one so…"

He couldn't decide on the next word he wanted to use. So he moved on.

"Blair, taking the lead against those… bastards. He was born in Scotland, you know?" he looked up hopefully.

"Those heroes. And you know, your Auntie Isobel said they had the flag at the fire brigade headquarters in Edinburgh at half mast for weeks… solidarity wi their brothers ower here…"

Quickly, however, the topic changed again.

"And now they want us all to use a new currency. Can you believe it? What am I gaunnae do about my bank account back in Inverkeithing? What's gaunnae happen to ma money? All this stuff about some bridges and buildings and windows that arenae anywhere."

I had completely lost track of what on earth he was rambling on about by this stage.

"I dinnae mind your curries or your pasta or your pizzas or your kebabs. That's all fine."

Like mom had dared feed him a pizza lately? I don't think so.

"There's just nae need tae change what's there." And I nodded slowly in response. "You know?"

That was one of the signs he wasn't on the far side of his alcoholic corner yet. He switched over into using the word "ken", which is the same as "know", only when seriously affected by liquor. It was still the early part of the afternoon, and it was a cup of tea he'd just finished.

"And those extra hundred-and-whatever-it-is new politicians they've got over there now. What good can they be doing? Eh? Eh?"

He was getting pretty animated. The usual round-robin set of topics, most of which I didn't understand at all at the time. Perhaps, I remember speculating, he would pass out any second, like the time the previous year, when he was sitting in the back of the Buick and the dirt road up the hill had been blocked. He had sprung out and had tried to shift the fallen tree with his bare hands but, without warning, just as he took hold of one of the branches, he keeled over backwards, landing on the road flat on his back, like the old tree had nailed him with some invisible upper cut the rest of us hadn't noticed.

"There's a building in Glasgow now that's like a tortoise. Oh!"

And those were the last words Uncle Andy ever spoke. Strangely poetic, I now think. I can still remember hearing the rotten crack of the wood and seeing his disappearing red face. I recall noticing how surprisingly smooth the soles of his shoes were as they swung up into the air, the legs of his loose pants flapping around the panicked, white-haired limbs before the back of the chair and Uncle followed the broken timber into the water with a protracted series of splashes.

I kept completely still in my seat, waiting patiently for the waves to lap up onto the stones at the water's edge. His hand thrashed above the surface just once, and there was a little bit of movement for five seconds or so under the water, which made the chair bob irregularly as it bumped around on top of him.

I scanned the lakeshore in both directions before craning my neck behind me to check the upstairs windows. I could just make out the beat of the music on the radio inside. But no head visible.

After pausing for ten seconds more, I stood up and walked into the house. Mom was coming down the stairs with a paintbrush in her hand. She must have done at least half the front bedroom by now, I figured.

"Are you okay, honey? Same old stories from Uncle Andy, huh?"

"Never tire of 'em," I chuckled. "Can I take out a pitcher of water?"

"Why, sure – there's no need to ask. Are you hungry? There's some muffins left."

"No thanks – it's okay."

"Does Andy need anything?"

"He said he'll maybe have some more tea later, but not now."

I filled the jug. Then, as I was about to leave the kitchen, Mom screamed at a volume that made me jump. "Oh my God, the jetty! What's happened to Andy?"

"Huh… Oh my God," I put my hand up to my mouth. "He was sitting there just a moment ago."

"It's crazy. Look at…"

"My God. It's broken. It must have happened just after I came inside. I don't believe it."

"Oh, Amy," Mom said. She ran out of the house and headed down to the water's edge. Watching out of the window, I could see her leaning over the newly splintered end of the pier and fishing around with her arms. I was kind of startled when she swung her legs round and jumped in the lake, but I guess we couldn't have left him lurking around in there.

Eventually, she reached the grass bank, her right arm around his surprised-looking, flabby body. She looked up at me through the window, with a blank sort of expression – I remember it pretty clearly. But I was just a kid with no brothers, sisters or cousins, thinking about all the cool stuff I could get with a five-figure sum. She didn't look like she especially needed my help anyhow.

She heaved him up onto the grass with a great burst of effort, after which she stepped out of the lake herself, breathing rapidly.

I felt the urge to go back outside and join her. I made my way down the lawn, and she came up to hug me.

Andy wasn't completely out of the lake, in fact – his legs were still partly immersed, one shoe slowly floating away to join the flotilla of timber fragments – but with the bulk of him now on the lawn, water streaming off in all directions, he at least wasn't going to go anywhere. I flinched in reaction to the coldness of Mom's wet clothes. She was shaking.

I looked over at Uncle Andy. It was as if he was sunbathing on the grass, cooling his feet in the water. Mom had made sure his head was turned so that it faced the other way.

She went inside and washed her hands, and I followed. "I'm going to try and reach your father, although he's probably still in his meeting," she said, picking up the phone. "Maybe you want to go up to your room and... or... or maybe phone Rosalind and see if she wants to come play or... or... maybe better ask if you can go over to..." and she started sobbing.

"It's okay, Mom," I said, hugging and surprising her, no longer concerned about the wetness of her clothes.

After that, I thought it was best to stay in my room for a while and let the situation be.

EARSHOT

So rare these days I get to go to a game. Delighted. Absolutely delighted. Nothing that special, though – just against the Inverness. It's a league game, so they'll not beat us like they tend do in the cup.

Usually have to be on standby at weekends in case work want me to go to Edinburgh or Manchester or Aberdeen. Only have to actually hop on a train about four or five times a year, though. Fine by me. Just means I can't plan tap all for Saturdays.

Bit of a silly standby arrangement to be absolutely honest, as I don't tire of hinting to Maxie. The extra day's half pay is much appreciated, of course, but personally I'd rather they used some more junior people and let them have their turns in the Away Shop, as we like to refer to it.

But not too junior. For our sort of clients, you don't put somebody too fresh-faced behind the desk, Glasgow or elsewhere. If they're too eager to prove themselves, that usually means they're the wrong type for it. Silk ties and confident answers to all questions – that's basically it. No hesitations or repetitions. The punters I see during the week are reasonably relaxed when they're sitting in front of me, to be fair, and strangely unchallenging in their questions more often than not, but they want discretion and trust above all. Banter? They want a wee bit of banter, for sure, but respecting the appointment time and sticking to the business in hand is always the best policy. Oh aye, one more thing: the cufflinks help a great deal. You can never underestimate the I'm-not-fucking-around-here effect of a pair of top-quality cufflinks – that's another certainty in life.

Pleasant as weekends at home are, and much as I love the quality time with the cat – and I do – it's nice when these little quirks of the rota give me the chance to come and go as I please for once. And Paradise is easy to get to from here.

Hoof it round the corner to Hyndland station. Pure love this station. Sky always blue, trees in most directions, regular trains of the electrical variety, people shuffling about quietly with no hurry, no fuss.

Train comes and me and a handful of other Cellic fans get on. "to make your hearts go" and all that goes through my head. I always take a scarf and it's always clean. There's people chatting, bantering away about the last few games, and nobody has a care in the world.

Loads of people get on at Queen Street low level, of course. There's one guy in particular, with a flat square face and black greasy tapes of hair, which look like they've been trimmed by a madman with a pair of kitchen scissors, adhering to the right-angled limits of his forehead. Probably mid-twenties, but with the uneven, wispy facial growth of a 15-year-old. Starts singing some Provo song I haven't heard in a wee while, with a whine at the edge of his voice and a roving, lolling movement of his head, craving everyone around him to join in. Unsuccessfully. Then he tries the more familiar ditty, bashing the window with his fist three times as he does "that stood – with – me". One or two mouth the words but nobody joins in really, and most look away, a bit pathetically. Some guy in his 50s with wavy Brylcreemed hair leans over and nudges me and says, "Agent provocateur."

Don't think much of the sandwich I've made myself, which is a bit pitiful, I must admit. Think to myself, Mikey, you'll shortly be having a pie, and you know it.

Glad I'm not inclined to leave it til the last minute before heading for the turnstiles, like so many fellow customers, who'll still be trotting along the Gallowgate past St Mungo's by kick-off time. Janefield Street – what's left of it – can get slightly too frantic for my liking. Speaking of which, one punter's lying flat out at the bottom of a green metal pillar near the corner of the north stand. From the split second I get to glance at his face, I can see he looks completely calm. He offers a casual unconsciousness to his transient audience, with a nonchalant bleeding, leaving the tense discussion with the police to the people around him. Good – it's always best to delegate when you're feeling poorly.

At 2.40 pm the queue's not too long yet – it will be in another three minutes, of course. My ticket is ripped into two, and I unsuccessfully bounce off the floor-to-ceiling turnstile once before the catch is released and I can feed myself into the stadium, which is filling up nicely with people who have paid an awful lot of money to witness a routine yet adequately hefty pummelling of an amalgamated Highland League XI playing in red and blue.

As I proceed I'm pondering the new customer I had on Tuesday morning, thinking about the impressive size of the deal for a first timer, wondering if it'll just be a one-off, despite the fat bugger's assurances to the contrary.

I go up the first flight of steps and throw my Welsh-inscribed pound coin into the skinny white hand of a Lisbon Lions Lottery ticket seller, who wishes me luck in an absurd American-imported gesture of service culture. It will be won an hour or so later by a white-headed man in a black Puffa jacket with a clean-looking green and white scarf, much like my own, who will look both chuffed and embarrassed, wondering what Monday's going to be like with all his new-found friends in the workshop.

I spot the staircase that'll take me to the correct bit of the upper tier. Piss. Pie queue. Then I'm standing there in a state of sudden doubt, wondering if I shouldn't get some dogburger instead. Get a funny sort of tap from behind. Not a tap. Almost a dig, four fingers pushing into the muscle at the top of my right shoulder. Pretty puzzled by this, so I'm frowning, scowling even, as I turn round. And there's this silly smiling face behind me. A face known to me, with a daft, infectious smile. I chuckle as I cooperatively give John Carter a soft punch in the chest.

"Special occasion, Mikey? Surprised no tae see the Jungle here, are ye?"

"Nice to see you, Johnny-bag. In the market for a pie?"

"If yer buyin."

"Pleasure," I say. "Ya cheap fuck," I add – perhaps overdoing the intimacy some.

"How's work?" I ask after we each take a big breath of stadium air – neither cold outdoors nor warm indoors, and neither full nor absent of cooking fat.

"Awright," says Carter, looking pleased, "Got a decent chance of promotion thair. Board's a week on Wednesday," he informs me.

"Mm hmm. Very good," I respond. I confess my lack of recent attendance and say something vague about business trips and so on. I purchase a pie and a cheeseburger, the latter being for myself. I take my sachet of brown sauce and hold it up to my face for a moment, contemplating it with a gimlet eye and a thoughtful frown like it might just turn out to be the key to eternal happiness. It surely won't be, but the thing would be inedible without it.

Then, as we enter the arena, he hits me with the bloody thing I've been trying to forget about today. "So, the old man's in a bit of a pickle, I see. Any truth in it? Or is the *Daily Chronicle* barking up the wrong turd?"

"Cheers," I respond. "Where abouts do you sit?"

He points to where his season ticket is allocated, a good dozen rows back, and I work out where my ticket is telling me to go. There's one empty seat to the left of my place, although it's a bit restricted because of an enormous man one along, but there are three more spaces to the right. Carter, who is becoming increasingly less welcome in the unfolding of my day, dumps himself down next to me, and we both start unwrapping our food as the players behave much more conscientiously, with everyone running about and stretching or practising the kicking of balls, except Magnus Hedman, who is trying to catch the things.

A few minutes later, just as the players come back out the tunnel and get into their now sacrosanct huddle, some dobber turns up and demands – reasonably, we both concede – to sit in his seat, so Carter ends up clambering into the empty place immediately in front of me, to the vivid annoyance of the adjacent couple in their mid-thirties.

O! how easy it once was, in a time now long ago, to shuffle away to avoid farts and bastards.

"I don't take the *Chronicle* these days, John," I say just after the Inverness boys kick off.

I lean forward to elicit his question. "£400,000 of EU funding disappearing into a bank account with your old man's name on it? What's he playing at?"

I react with impeccable candour by shrugging. "Well, it's what he's been doing with it that would be more interesting to the likes of you I suspect."

"What?" goes Carter, bracing his facial muscles to have a good giggle.

I stoop forward, putting one hand on the back of his seat and almost resting my chin on his shoulder. "It's been kindly brought to my attention that the Lapwing Club is pretty much being kept going these days by the old boy's new-found collection of £10 notes," I say above the noise of the crowd reacting to Didier Agathe quickening his pace.

Johnny-bag twists his head back to face me and registers genuine astonishment, pursing his lips at the same time as he opens his mouth, which makes it a marvellous egg shape. His gaze bobs up to the roof of the stand. "Head of major enterprise company resigning in scandal... that's got to be about the first third of 'Reporting Scotland' on an otherwise quiet day, hasn't it?"

I smirk at him, making sure I keep his eye contact for a good few seconds. "Thanks to you? Surely not, now."

Carter raises his eyebrows and scratches the side of his face. It is an apt time for Celtic to make their break into the box and slot home what turns out to be the only goal of the game, annoyingly early. Some people in my row don't even bother standing up.

"Thirty percent okay?" J asks. Don't quite get what he means for a few seconds.

"What?"

"Papers."

"Papers? Ah… Anything but the *Chronicle*."

"The *R*—"

"Sshh! I cannae hear you."

And he turns back round to face the front again.

Don't know what it is about them, but I love Thursdays almost as much as I love weekends. You've really got the week by the balls by the Thursday morning. Monday's a farce, Tuesday's wrist-slashing time, Wednesday means going over the top and lobbing a few grenades, but Thursday... Thursday is rich and Thursday is good. It's when by far the best deals are done. It's when you're on top form, precisely because you're just starting to tire. Your mind is dulled, so a fraction of concentration is distilled into a fraction of lucid thinking. And that's when your performance peaks.

I've made myself a bloody fantastic lunch this time, having informed a Mr Owen Baker not only that I'll be happy to take care of his personal finances – in my own rather special way – but that my ace colleague and champagne buddy, Alexis (Jesus loves her but He knows fine well that's not her real name), can look after his nice young wife's interests.

It's a quarter to one. I kick my office door closed and unleash the until now Tupperware-gagged smell of the richest, most perfect egg mayonnaise this side of Falkirk. I'll grab a cappuccino from downstairs shortly – fuck it, let's make it a latte – and the perfection of my world will be thus consolidated.

As I glance at the day's press pile, I feel rather as if I'm sitting in the club deck of a transatlantic airline, with all the comforts you could possibly want on your way to the Big, lovely Apple, but then realising that the pilot has suddenly decided to flip the plane over and fly upside down.

Then I take a nice, deep breath.

I am struck first by the photos accompanying the article, which are imaginatively chosen and captioned. Part of the piece mentions the girls being totally discrete, but I suspect a lot of the details might well have come from them anyway. Focusing heavily on the "spotted leaving" ploy, it's well researched and the series of links from the funding office in Brussels is explained through the use of a handy map, with plenty of arrows, a close-up of central Glasgow and some numbers. It's a good bit of hack-work.

I thrum my fingers for a few seconds and then flick my eyes through the text a second time, making sure there aren't any hidden journalistic dogturds with my own initials on them. Nope. The pilot flips the plane the right way up again, and I dream of New York, with a transposed Times Square flashing and pumping its energy up the road from the end of Gordon Street. I practically go down on my egg roll, looping bits of white with the end of my tongue, savouring the yolk as I extrude it.

I'll do a spot of shopping on the way home: cat food and the indigestion tablets I'll need tonight when my bout of nerves kicks in after the time lag. I lick the egg off the sides of my teeth and dispose of the balled-up clingfilm with a misdirected drop-kick, mouthing "We don't care what the animals say" as I punch my fist and grit my teeth in a little war dance.

And I drink that latte like it's the blood of my fathers. And then there's the ring-tone and my actual one's phone number popping up on the wee grey screen. His interest in my investment services has been uncannily keen of late, and I can only imagine he'll be grateful for the chance to speak to me again.

today's condiment flash fiction

"He had a wee sachet of salad cream in his top pocket. That's where the bullet hit. Hence the bits ay salad cream mixed in wi the blood and everything else."

"But... did it save him?"

"No."

aphorisms and musings (ii)

62. In the strangers' country, people may be equally offended by your confession that you (a) imagined they lived in great comfort with modern amenities or (b) imagined they did not live in comfort or have modern amenities.

63. Is a bing still a bing if it is located outwith Scotland?

64. Is the universe here for a purpose?
For most people in the world, the answer is yes, because cause and effect on its own, without purpose, is psychologically intolerable. Theological explanations have therefore been required so as to supply intelligence that is capable both of reasoning and of performing tasks beyond the capabilities of human beings and before their existence.
For a minority of people in the world, it's a no. Cause and effect (albeit incompletely explained) is generally adequate to account for things not determined by human beings, and the idea of reason itself long pre-dating the intelligent life that is capable of reasoning (ours or any other) is a logical absurdity.

65. Is there any point at all pretending that we live in a civilised society when individual people choose to ignore some of the rules?

66. It is a necessary curse in life that such a small minority of people have great bums.

67. It is an inevitable cultural result of the trans-hemispheric migration of their predominantly European ancestors that Australians know more than Europeans do about the Coriolis effect.

68. It is August 2011, and parts of London have been burning and getting smashed up. It occurs to me that both the inequality of capitalism and the attempted equality of socialism (and many other approaches) require rules and barriers in order to function, in as much as they do. These will always be challenged and, sometimes, broken by people who feel themselves to be on the wrong side of them and to have been disadvantaged by the regime to which they are subject. Hence, in the absence of any system under which all human animals can feel content, there will always be riots and revolutions in some places and under some circumstances.

The barriers broken in this instance include shop windows, which separate valuable goods from the masses. The social barriers to obtaining them are formed using highly differentiated rights to obtain money, such that the availability of these goods is greater among the wealthier, more privileged groups. The physical barrier is glass, which is the more corporeal restraint mechanism, but it can be broken by members of the more impoverished, socially excluded groups (and of course anyone else who feels like joining in the fun), using bricks, concrete, boots and fire. Some of these young people have observed that they are able to get and do what they want today. The idea that they might be right, together with the obvious fact that the police cannot possibly be expected to control the behaviour of many hundreds of looters and rioters acting simultaneously and unpredictably in multiple locations, shocks the bourgeoisie.

69. It is both more effective and more acceptable to treat individuals as if they are intelligent and the collective as if they are stupid.

70. It is Britain in the 1990s. Everywhere, pubs have television sets on with the sound turned off and completely unrelated music playing at the same time. It just goes to show that national trends are often started and spread by imbeciles with really stupid fucking pointless senseless moronic and did I mention stupid and pointless ideas.

71. It is necessary to be simultaneously considerate and assertive when assisting somebody who is vomiting through alcoholic excess.

72. It is still through our own free will that we are another's puppet.

73. It must take an overwhelming degree of self-assurance to wish to procreate.

74. It provokes a particularly tragic exasperation to come upon a pedestrian crossing at a busy junction, with about 20 people waiting to cross, and not one of them has thought to press the button. Words almost fail me.

75. It's a surprising thing, but you really have to watch when you purchase a doughnut in a culture with which you are not familiar. I was on holiday once on a small island in the Atlantic and I ate the worst goddamn doughnut ever.

76. It's only because you feel vulnerable that you need to put them down.

77. It's rude to disbelieve people.

78. Just keep looking, and you'll find that tie you quite like but haven't worn for ages.

79. Laws and rules are most definitely there to be adhered to – the exception arising in the case of a revolutionary consensus.

80. Laws are the discourse of the empowered.

81. Literature is the contract of thought.

82. Look, Girard, I simply refuse to admit that so much of my activity is mimetic – and I'm exactly like other people that way.

83. Love, anger and grief are just three recognisable shades of the singular madness that sets us apart from the robots.

84. Love's greatest gift is understanding.

85. Microwaving food that has no microwaving instructions on the packaging is the zenith of convenience eating.

86. Most things are forgivable.

87. Need attracts disappointment.

88. Nice boys just go about being bastards in a more passive way.

89. Nineties technology had a small number of buttons doing many things; eighties technology had quite a few things done by a great many very small buttons; seventies technology had a few great big knobs and switches to do a couple of things.

90. Nobody is truly altruistic; there are people, however, who are good at practising altruism.

91. [*Withdrawn, as a creepy and untrue generalisation about **women** and **men***].

92. Nuthin scunners fowk like an unexpectit act ay kindness.

93. Of all the possibly correct answers to that highly invasive question, "What are you thinking?" the response "Thinking a great deal about Shakira" is <u>not</u> one of them.

94. OK, I admit it. I enjoy drinking cold water out of used beer bottles.

95. One must simply be brave on discovering that all the salt and vinegar crisps have sold out at the petrol station.

96. One of the rare aspects of life that men and women experience identically is the periodic need for Bonjela.

97. One's response to pleasure is the same as that to hardship: surrender.

98. Other people have slippers.

99. Our species actually does rather well with enough love, nourishment and education.

100. People are pathetic; men are particularly pathetic.

101. People, not the laws that they make, are the true arbiters of what is and is not permissible.

102. People tend to look for an answer before considering whether or not there is likely to be one at all. They do so foolishly.

103. People who are generally poor at lying are exceptional at it in exceptional circumstances.

104. People who complain about having a lot of small change on them are idiots.

105. Politics only exists because no political model works effectively.

106. Power compromises the powerful.

107. Puppies are fluffy and cute. They shit.

108. Putting others first. Great for being Jesus or a good citizen; a disaster for the ambitious male heterosexual.

109. Remember the departed; cuddle the living.

110. Revenge is a dish best served cold, so you might as well have some potato salad at the same time.

111. Rules generally apply to everybody in a jurisdiction. That said, everybody, through free will, has the ability to exempt themselves from any of these rules, should they wish to, at any time of their choosing.
(with thanks to the fellow cyclist who breezed past me and proceeded through the red light onto Torphicen Street this morning, a man whose open contempt for his fellow human beings deserves repeated punching in the face, and perhaps something additional to annoy him that I can't quite think of at the moment)

112. Sarcastically saying how tasty the sprig of parsley on top of the bowl of potatoes is – or leaping onto the table with a short skirt and no pants on, clutching a vibrator and screaming, "Who can do it? Who can do it?" – it always depends on the precise degree to which you want to shock your host.

113. Secretly, leading astrophysicists prefer the term 'wee dot' to 'singularity'.

114. See how the rebel grows older and cherry-picks the tree of the Establishment.

115. Smaller, more remote towns experience a slower pace of change compared with large cities. How fondly I remember my holiday visits to the little town of M—. As recently as 2000, there were two charming posters in the chip shop there. The first, from the Potato Marketing Board, urged us to accompany our fish with chips. What an idea! The second, from the British Fish Association, suggested that we might accompany our chips with fish. Not least because of its disastrous late-1990s advertising campaign built around the slogan "They're not all horrible", the BFA is now defunct.

116. Society is mass self-control.

117. Some people are so interesting they're about as interesting as two people.

118. Such is the balance of power in Scotland at the commencement of the millennium: tabloid newspapers' control of the country is messy and indirect, involving as it does cycles of ministers, party leaders and the like, not to mention the palaver of universal adult suffrage. Instead, editorials should simply be transposed into statute by celebrity draftsmen, with the selection of new laws proportionate to readership, and with all the behind-the-scenes documentary opportunities regulated by Holyrood's Subordinate Legislation Committee.

119. Thanks to the distorting experience of film and television viewing, many people now believe that they cannot be overheard by a third party standing 10 feet away from them.

120. The atheist believes he has no-one to thank for what others call blessings. Nonetheless, he feels it important to voice his gratitude for his child's brief sweet life.

121. The best things in life are free. And often pens.

122. The common law and statute to which we are subject exists because of certain similarities in patterns among the chemical and electrical impulses that are experienced by influential bunches of organic molecules.

94

123. The cretinously stupid tendency of people to keep pressing pedestrian crossing or elevator buttons when they are clearly already lit up is a vivid demonstration of the failure of our nation's education methods.

124. The day the cup of tea is no longer seen as a panacea is the day all vestiges of British Imperial civilisation finally end.

La manutention de l'infini

or

The Unspeakable

The visor closes again
Rectangular and round
Contorted bedroom parkscape
No colours; inner sound.

The convex park, the wooden fence, grass pitches
Distant hedges
The mounds of sand on the far side
The disappearing edges.

It has started.
No eyes nor teeth nor mouth
Voice from a shapeless armoured head
Commands me to look at every point.
No interruption of the stretch in front
As far as I can see and further.

Hypnosis must give rise to things unique.
The nightmare lets me touch what cannot be.
These stocky hands constrict my chest
Lid of my brain forced open
With thick matchsticks
Forced to see what daily consciousness shuts out
Half awake
Amid the black ocean, battened on my bed.
The sky too wide
It does not end.
And this is the horror:
Squares and lines and numbers make space countable.

To count the never ending
Leads you there
To tears and breakdown
And panicked hope of retreat.

The overloaded cortex tries to grip
The vast numbers that pulp organic calculations
And squeeze the juice, turning buoyant grey matter
To sticky dry fear.
A nauseating fall
Through tiny bubble tracts of emptiness.
Unseeable lumpen lack of face.
Void-substance pushed up to the corners of the room.
No air left to breathe.
Mind borne through infinite outer space
Onto the horizon of a

Jute sack
That carries within it
The volume
Of a large gas planet unseen and unseeable
While the jute-bagged child drowns deliriously in the blue sea,
        just a mile from the shore.

Infinity would be easy
But the finite number of all the world's building blocks
Is a possibility vaster than the impossible

The rhythmless counting leads to sickness
Voice fills dark
Dark drives fear
Fear without escape
Or remedy
Except the morning.

The size of the moon's orbit
Strains the inner space behind the eyelids
Black alone is deep enough to suffocate
Size is minuscule and vast
The brain is feeble and cowering
Yet unavoidably charged with the administration of a nebula of stars
And each and every one of their atoms
Help
Help the perspective-tortured one
Cramped and stuck in boundless spacetime
Stargazing from the bottom of a well whose circumference is the equator.

4 am. Rescuing daylight is too far away to hail yet
So turn over and cry
Eyes locked open in lead-lined sleep
And beg for mercy

Which is bestowed in time.
For after the endless dark,
Perhaps too late,
Perhaps not,
Morning answers
And mothers you into the day's sweet, bright life.

TO THE MOON

"It says here," reported Maude, "David Beckham wants to go to the moon."

David (that's David Denton, not David Beckham) was genuinely taken aback by this news, and it was a few seconds before he replied,

"Really?"

Although he wasn't so struck by it that he felt the need to look up from his own newspaper, which was not too far from his wife's on the socio-political spectrum.

"Yeah," Maude said, in that slightly distant voice that comes out of people who are mainly concentrating on reading and only fractionally on summating the information to the other person. "He says it would be an interesting experience."

"He's still got a couple of years left in the Real Madrid first team, though, I would think," commented David. "Maybe more. But now he says he wants to go to the moon, you say. I didn't think they had a team up there yet. Perhaps somebody's told him otherwise," David added, snorting.

David had lost concentration now. "Would you like to go to the moon, Maude?"

Maude stared contemptuously towards him, but her gaze was blocked by, and she found herself instead focusing on, a picture of Saddam Hussein looking miffed with no clothes on. "A bit dangerous, isn't it?" she almost snarled.

"There's always Uzbekistan…" muttered David, having turned the page.

Maude hated these non-answers.

"Hey," said David, suddenly sitting up and lowering his newspaper.

"Hey," he repeated, staring to chuckle, to Maude's irritation.

"Wh – " David started laughing.

"Who… ha ha ha ha ha ha ha ha… Who… ha ha ha ha ha – "

And he couldn't go on. Maude found herself smiling in response to this display of mirth, and was consequently furious with herself.

"He – He – he he he… Oh. oh. oh."

He was shaking up and down now, and was starting to cry, and coughing. His whole body was rocking about.

He let go of the newspaper, which fell onto his knees. The middle pages started to slide, one by one, down his legs.

"Ha… aaaaah…" he went, uncontrolled, his creased eyelids closed, his arms resting on the armrests, each hand clenching and unclenching arrhythmically.

"Ooh! Ooh ooh oh ho ho ha ha ha ha ha. Ah! Ah! Aaaah…"

He could barely breathe now.

"Does he…" he managed. "Ha! Haaaaa! Aaaah!" David shouted.

"Oh! Ohhh! Ooooh…Oh! Oh! Does he… Does he want… Oh God."

He lowered his head, blowing and sucking air between his lips.

"Oh Jesus."

David was nearly spent.

"Does he…" he said more quietly. Then he said "Does heeee…" again, but in a strangled, hysterical screech.

Finally, after taking a deep breath and dabbing some tears from his eyes with the back of his hand, he expressed the question to his wife, calmly and quietly.

"Does he want to play for Moon United, then?" David asked her.

Several seconds of silence.

He was trembling, his big red face covered in perspiration, as if he'd gone mad.

Something in Maude was, she acknowledged, a little bit amused. But she was certainly not going to join David in this display of idiocy. And just then, he started roaring again, not so much laughing, exactly, as repeatedly shouting out the word "Ha".

Maude returned with a cup of tea for each of them. David had now left his armchair and was kneeling on the floor, wetness dripping off his face. He was beating the carpet with his fists, going

"Wooooh. Woooh. Hoooo. Moon!"

He tried to look up but his eyes were flooded with tears. He managed to raise his right hand, pointing up towards the ceiling.

"To the moon! To the mooooooooon… hee hee hee hee hee hee hee hee."

Maude set the tea tray down, switched on the television and took her first sip, having decided just to ignore her husband for the next little while.

CLERICAL, IS IT?

I went in, yeah, and, like, the guy – he was quite nice and had a really sweet Irish voice on him – says, "Clerical, is it, now?" I didn't know what else it would have been, so I says, "Yeah, please, thank you," whatever, and I takes the form and sits down with it at a table. Table's too low of course, so I just do it on a magazine on my knee, don't I?

It's just the same as the rest of them, and I've got my CV with me so I fills it out easy, with all my last jobs in order, and I use the BT one and the Sun Alliance one a lot for the experience section, because of the fact of what I did there, yeah?

So I fills them out, real quick I did.

And, actually, there's not too many people there, being a Tuesday, and so he goes to me, "That's fine, Ms Reid, do you have time to complete a typing and data entry test today?" and I look at my watch and say, like I'm maybe thinking about it, but I'm not, yeah, "Yes, yes, that's no problem," so he's, you know, "Would you like to follow me," and when he sat down at this desk at the interview, you know, I sort of thought about him all, you know, coming on to me and undoing his tie and saying stuff, yeah. Funny, yeah.

Not serious – don't get me wrong or nothing. Idle thoughts, is what you'd call it. I have got a boyfriend.

I got 35 on the typing and, you know, they don't care if it's just two-finger. Got really high on the data entry. Six thousand something. Same test as all the rest. Some geezer must have made a packet, selling these little lists of addresses and numbers to every temping agency in London, yeah?

In the interview I'm pretty cool. I say what I did before and just, like, get fairly blasé, not *really* blasé, of course, about my office experience and

I convinces him without any bother and it looks like I'm onto a score pretty soon because he says, "There is one position that came up yesterday, in fact," he says, so, yeah, it looks pretty good.

"Report to Martin Jonk at 8.45am – security pass to be issued on second day – Mr Jonk will sign you in on mornings of first two days." That's what the writing on the introduction card says, yeah?

Jonk, you know. It's not a common name but it's probably German, yeah? Maybe Holland, yeah? Horses for courses.

I meets this Jonk, and he is English. Don't know if his mother's from, you know, Holland, yeah, but I don't ask. Actually, it's maybe his father, because it's his surname that's Dutch or whatever. Maybe it's his mother that's English. Search me, yeah?

I'm surprised I have to wear a namebadge, but it's for 'staff recognition', apparently. I'm still surprised, yeah, because it's calls, mainly. I explain that my real name's Edding Reid and they say my name's Edwina on the form, well they didn't say, you know, they asked, and I said that Edwina is what it is on official forms mostly.

Edwina's what it is on my passport, which is great, cos if I'm, you know, on the run or something, they maybe, like, won't find out my real name.

It's better than the last job because the calls are all streamed and it's only really simple inquiries from people who've already decided to buy equipment and they've been transferred down from Sales. Well, our team is technically part of Sales, but we just process the order, it's them that make the sale, yeah, so we do say, like, "passed through from Sales." Horses for courses, really. Them lot work two floors upstairs, yeah?

It's only one and a half day's training before you take calls with a call buddy, yeah. I'm fine about it because, you know, I'm sort of confident, and it's just so much easier than my last job because that was really hard with all the different sorts of things people could ask you about, you know?

I'm finished at five if I want, but loads of people do an extra hour a day til six. Might as well do that most days, yeah? I live at home, in my flat.

Cassie's not smiling when I get in and she's not pleased. She's got this phone bill, you know, the one she spent Monday night de-itemising or working out, yeah, and she's, like, saying, "I sent the cheque off so I really need the money today or tomorrow cos if it comes out of my account before you've paid me your share then I'm shafted," cos she talks like that, yeah.

So I says she asked me last week and she gets all stroppy – she's, like, saying that's the whole point and the point is that she asked and I didn't do nothing and didn't pay and I can see where she's coming from but she doesn't really get it. I write her a cheque – I know which drawer I put my chequebook in, you see, I know it – and just give it to her. I think it'll clear cos the last time I saw Mum she gave me fifty, so I've not withdrawn cash – from the bank, yeah – for ages, or hardly anything anyway, and the pay'll start to come in soon I should think.

It's unbelievable, right: Paul, he's my other flatmate, yeah, he's cooking pasta and it's me that wants to cook – and cook pasta and all.

I says, "I'm cooking pasta, right," and he sort of replies, "No, like, I'm the one who's cooking pasta."

I just looks at him like I don't believe him. Yeah, he's got to eat I suppose, but why can't he wait like anyone else? He says I can put a saucepan next to his. Suppose.

His girlfriend's in another country, yeah. She's teaching in Spain, I think it is, and I fancy him, and he's available right now, and my boyfriend's not phoned, and, anyway, I really fancy him.

I don't tell him or nothing. I seen him in his pyjamas once – t-shirt and boxers, yeah? – and he's got a well amazing bod.

I cook the pasta and I make a sauce out of cheese and tomato sauce and flour. I find frozen peas too and put them in. Cassie says something like it's as good as what you'd get in a restaurant, an Italian restaurant, so I says yeah and I eats it. I go on the kitchen table, but Paul's watching the racing, the formula 1 highlights he recorded off the telly, so I says to him, "leave you to it" and I goes through to my room and I finish eating it there.

My tops and knickers and bras and socks are all on the line, cos I washed 'em, yeah. It's just as well, cos I ain't worked five-day weeks for a while and it takes a bit of getting used to and you need clean washing for it.

I brush my teeth with my orange toothbrush, cos it's newer than the grey one and it's got nicer bristles.

I'm feeling pretty up for it, quite honestly, and I think Paul's maybe gone to bed. I got condoms in my room, but he doesn't know I want to shag him yet, so I suppose I'll have to take mine into his room.

I wear my Miami Beach top, which comes half way down my thigh – nightshirt, yeah? – and underneath it's my green silk knickers and the purple velvety bra, not actual velvet, I don't think, although it might be, and I put Paul's aftershave he keeps in the bathroom all over my tits and down my knickers. You know why? Cos sometimes I think he loves himself.

I hope he likes me, cos I really want him and he's nice and he's free tonight.

It was really late when I decided to go through. Early, yeah? Two o'clock. I knew he'd be asleep. Hoped he'd be asleep. Better to be surprised, yeah?

I'm in my bare feet and I'm on the carpet just outside his door. It's soft. Warm. I can feel just the littlest draught coming from under his door. Must have a window open, yeah? Ventilation, yeah? His poster with a list of daft things Murray Wilson has said at racing commentary is on his door.

Wilson, Walker – horses for courses.

I open the door. He's asleep. Knew he'd be asleep, see? I close the door a little bit, not all the way, yeah? He rolls over, but I goes nearer him. He's got no t-shirt on. Phwoar. I gets nearer him, and he opens his eyes.

"Sandr…" he starts.

"Nuh, it's me, 'Dwina," I says, careful not to say my real name.

"Wha…?" he starts, then I just takes my bra off. Slips off me.

"It's time for your midnight treat," I says to him, and he just looks at me. His eyes are wide open and he's staring at my tits. I take the condom in the packet out the side of my knickers and I chuck it down on the carpet by his bed.

"I…" he starts, then I comes towards him and I take his left hand and make him feel me. He says oh god or something and I use my left hand to lift up the duvet and feel around a bit. He shivers, then I find what I'm looking for and I hardly need to touch it and it just grows really big. I move above him and let my boobs go on his face and he coughs a bit cos of his own aftershave, then I sit on him, and it makes me feel. I'm sitting on it, and its getting even bigger and he's starting to move, and his hands are shaking, but they're all over me. I start to feel something a bit more, and I look down at the shiny packet on the floor. I let myself relax and I kiss him, but then he sort of squirms and says can't do this or something. "Oh yes you can," I says, and I find under his boxer shorts again with my right hand and play a bit, and I really start kissing him. He says oh my god and you can't and no and stuff. I reach down and touch inside and then I put my finger to his nose so he can smell me. Then he opens his mouth, so I put my finger right in it. He's rather surprised, I think, and he makes a sort of Aah sound. Then I start to kiss him again.

He says you mustn't and I says I must, you know, like I'm answering him back, and then it goes wrong. He suddenly goes all red and sits up and asks me what the **** (I ain't gonna write what he says) I'm doing. I leans across to him and says to him, "you loved feeling my tits," and for a minute it looks like he's going to get back to giving us what we both want but for some reason he gets sort of cross (not as cross as at first, exactly) and says to me to go away and get back to my own bed and what I think I'm playing at and all that sort of stuff. I says, "OK, then," cos if he really don't want it it's not happening, yeah, obviously, but I'm a bit pissed off he doesn't want to kiss me. I'm only being sociable, yeah. And we do live together.

I gets back to bed, and, I'm being honest here, I'm a bit disappointed. Like I said, we must really fancy each other, but, I don't know. I'd never tell Sandra, and he'd never tell my boyfriend, yeah? So what's the... you know, yeah? I don't know. I can't work it out.

I do me, yeah?

Then I'm asleep, right? Catching a few Zs
Zees, zeds? Horses. Zebras.
And guess who comes in my bedroom at five fifty seven in the morning? Only Paul, yeah? He's wearing his blue dressing gown. He doesn't wear it round the flat much. Maybe on Sundays and stuff. Suits him, though: sexy, yeah? I sits up in bed, yeah, hardly believing my pork pies, and he comes towards me. So I lifts up the side of my duvet. "Lovely and warm under here," I says. He looks down and he can see one side of me. I'm wearing nothing. You know what he says? He says,

"Now, you've got to listen to me, Edwina, you really took me a bit by surprise earlier on and I was a bit confused: I was fast asleep and I was rather taken aback by your coming in like that. I'm still pretty shocked to be honest and... well, I'm even more shocked by my... Well, you're attractive, Edwina. There's no doubt about that, and I... I know it's been a long time since you've seen your boyfriend, but you can't go around... Look, Edwina, my relationship with Sandra means a lot to me and so does fidelity. If I went around... well, I'm not saying there's not a part of me that... But I think it's just silly to jeopardise a good relationship by being unfaithful.

"Edwina, I'm sorry, I've been awake for hours. It's just... please don't ever do something like that again and don't you dare tell a living soul, not Cassie, not any of your friends at work or anywhere else. This never happened. You will never ever ever ever do anything like that again. You will leave me alone and I will leave you alone. Although, of course, I hope we can remain good flatmates and... and good friends, of course.

"I'm sorry." And he goes back to his room, really.

So I don't know, do I?

Disappointed? I don't get disappointed, me.

So, I don't know.

I'm tired. I'm sort of feeling a bit randy again, cos, well he's got a real bod and it's been ages. I'll get an edge of the duvet.

I do have a boyfriend, though; it's just he hasn't been around. I don't care what I'm wearing or not wearing, I just go to sleep.

Night.

7 o'clock I wakes up again. Not very much later, really. I ain't got my top on, and it's lying by the bed. I reach for it cos I'm cold but it's all wet. Must have been sweating, whatever – and taken it off in my sleep, yeah? I'm sleepy. I don't like being awake this time of morning. Cigarette? No, I just falls asleep. Cigarettes? Fags? Most people try giving them up. I'm trying to start em again but I still don't like the taste much and can't get used to it. If it's not horses, it's courses, yeah?

It doesn't feel like a usual morning when I wake up again. There's something real thick about the air. It's – oh my god

Now I've opened my eyes I can see. I am breathing… but I can't be. I gets confused and I choke. I expect to be choking serious. Drowning even. But I'm really breathing. I'm breathing really.

It's blood, not air. That's why I says I can't be breathing. But I am.

It's quite dark, but I can see through it. I can see the window and the light coming in through it. There's little bubbles all the way through the blood. It's all red, obviously, yeah? They're not rising up, though, the bubbles, probably because the blood's too thick. Thicker than water, they say, although why they say it… They. They say so many things sometimes.

My hands can't move fast, yeah. Not like through air. Not like through water, either, yeah? I feel the side of the bed. It feels funny. I switch on the light by my bed and the button's all… Sort of.

I know. The blood's clotting on all the surfaces. It's forming solid mucky lumps on the corners of the bed, on the table, on the ashtray, on the window sill, yeah? I don't like it.

I don't like this, yeah? It's not nice. I'm still breathing, yeah, but I'm a bit worried, frankly, cos it doesn't make much sense.

I feel it's really important to reach the door. I wonder if all the blood will pour – ooze, yeah? – out through the doorway out into the hall. I'll dry off, but if I'm breathing now, what about then? What if I can't breath air, man? I'm a blood-breather, yeah? What if I can't fucking breath the fucking air, man? Fucking.

Air's not for me. I breathe blood soup. Dark red and life giving. I'm a haemogirl. Haemofuckingbaby.

I should still get out of this room, really, I think, so I goes to the door and try and open it. My hand sort of skids and I can't hold the doorknob. Fucking clotted up, innit? Couldn't probably get a key into the keyhole, I'm thinking, because of the clotted blood. Mind you, it's soft. Red snot, really, that's what it's like.

I push the door and it opens easy, just an inch or two. The next room's full of a different, clear, liquid, but it's only at waist height though my bedroom's full of blood up to the ceiling

bloody full of it

so that means – this is physics, yeah? – this blood stuff, loads of it, has to flow out of my room out into the hall. The level of the blood falls past me and I can feel air on the top of my head. I take one last gulp of blood, which is difficult because it's so thick. I have time to put my hand out into the gunge outside. It's clear, though, not red, yeah?

I go with the flow, yeah? Out into the hall, in the middle of the red stuff. But the blood's only up to my neck and what am I breathing now, man? What if FUCK! What if this clear stuff's just, like, pure nitrogen, and no oxygen? I need my haemowhack. Falling forward. I'm falling forward, cos I went and pushed the door open and kept leaning. All the weight off my feet and I can't control myself falling forward and

waking

up

in

my bed, covered and covered in sweat and the mattress is all sticky, and then I notice the massive stain under my bum. Disaster. What the fuck, yeah? Well early.

Paul's really nice in the morning. He puts his arm round me cos I said I had a headache and he pours me out a big bowl of cornflakes. He's real sweet, he is.

I'm on my way to work when I realise – now, I did know this when I left the flat, don't get me wrong, but I sort of *really knew it* once I'd got past the second set of traffic lights, yeah? – that I haven't really got my work clothes on.

They all just act like I'm not there most of the time, yeah? So it should be all right if I don't turn up til tomorrow. I go to the park instead.

There's no ducks on the pond. Don't know who took them away. Stupid really, no ducks on a duckpond. No swans or nothing.

I've just lit up a fag, haven't I, when this jogger almost knocks me in, he does, and I have to step on the little bit of grass just next to the water. Wanker.

Swans, ducks – horses for courses.

There's some man with a leather jacket on the other side of the pond looking at me. Got a kid with him. He's dead cute, throwing bread into the water. There's a duck on the far side. I just didn't see it before. I got a sore head. The kid's got curly blond hair and he's looking at his daddy, who's still looking over at me – well, thought he was. He's not any more. Wanker.

It's past ten o'clock. Shit. What if someone says "Where's Dwina?" at work. Shit.

Still, it's OK, cos I'm here at the pond, so what can they do anyway? Like I says, it don't make no difference when I'm in the office – everyone just carries on. Regardless, yeah?

I got a sore head, so I sits down on a bench. No old tramps here or anything. There is sometimes though. I can't really see the far side, but I don't know why that is cos I don't need specs or anything. The sky's not right and it starts to feel really warm. I'm

oh shiiiiiiiiiiiiitttt what's happening?

I'm really starting to feel sick, yeah? I wish the sky would stop moving.

I look behind me and, I don't know, it's gone all dark.

I feel a lot warmer now. I look behind me.

I can't see the water any more at all. It's like the pond's sort of invisible, yeah? But I still know exactly where I am.

I'm warm. I look behind me. It's like a hood.

No, it's all right, it's mine. This is where I am. The clouds are fluffy, and the whole sky's sort of wobbling a little bit.

Pushed along, pushed along.

I can't see the pond – at least I don't think I can see it. I'd have to sit up, that's for sure.

And then I realise I don't know how to yet. Shit!

Along. Along.

This face comes over the side. Hello, mum.

Mum's smiling. Here comes her hand. She's playing with my cheek. Thanks, Mum, I like that. I give her a big smile. But where's my dummy gone?

Then we go again. We'll be at the shops next. I hope she gets me an ice lolly. I like lollies. It's been too long since I last had one, and I'm desperate for one. Nice fruity one, preferably, not one of those milk ones.

It's getting dark.

It is dark.

Hello, Mum.

Eddie

naC uoy raeh em? yhW's enoyreve gnikaeps sdrawkcab? yhW? Whyyhwwwwhyyyyyy?

Why? yhW? – sesroh rof sesruoc.

Hello Eddie.

Obviously this bit must be a bit later, yeah?
Mum.
Can you hear me, Eddie?
Mum.
Oh, Eddie.
Mum.
Edwina?
Mum?
No, I'm the doctor.
Mick. I can see Mick.
Dwina? Can you really see me? Long time, no see.
Mick, I… where's that doctor gone?
Here I am, Edwina.
Edwina, you've got to listen to the doctor now.
Can you remember what drugs you've been taking?
Sorry? Wouldn't be good drugs if I could still remember,
I say.
Edwina!
No. I don't do drugs, Mum, doctor. Mick? Mick, tell em I don't do
drugs, yeah?… Yeah. Headache, though, yeah?
I'm so sorry, Mrs Reid.
Then nothing.
Then lots of shouting and my mum's upset.
I don't really get it, yeah. I'm not dead or nothing, I hope. That would
bloody explain a lot, though.
Actually, no it wouldn't.
I should be at park. Work, yeah?
What was it? Eh? What was it?
She's asked that before.
She won't ask it again. I think. Don't know, really.
I want to go back.
I want to go back and I want everything to be OK.
And most of all I want to go back.
Help, Mum.

I took my slippers

1992. It was an obvious thing to do.
And it started well enough.

We shopped efficiently in the Wm Low
For sausages, beans and butter.

First, a detour at my insistence
Around the geometrically defined library pond
Including the sticky-out boardwalk bits.
Milngavie resident clocked us with our Karrimor rucksacks.
She leaned out of her window,
Insisting we were going the wrong way.
I didn't explain the childhood nostalgia thing
For the library and its pond.

Lasagne and a pie at Dumgoyne,
Too much ankle-deep mud on the old railway,

Then his gastroenteritis, developed with uncanny haste.
The farmer didn't approve of campers,
Judging from the Land Rover lights trained on our tent
In the middle of the night,
And the sporadic gunfire.
He was violently sick
And more,
And trod in a cowpat in his bare feet.
I was in hysterics.
Ill-slept, we noted in the morning light
How the nearby landscape was now garnished
With his vivid rejections of yesterday's lunch.

1993. Thanks be to God, this time he
Restricted his gastric violence in Drymen
To two considered visits to the pub toilet.
But after dark, new threats emerged on last year's field:
Grass ripped from the ground,
Chomped in terrifying proximity,
A whole flock of cows circling the tent.

If one of these invisible lumbering
Spectres of the night tripped over a guy rope,
Came breenging in through the canvas,
It would kill us both.
A premature crushing of hopeful life.

The ugly people were waiting at Rowardennan.
My god.

The next night, it was the slugs.
A tight-knit gang of them, gallus,
Gave us a cheeky morning welcome.
One of them refreshed after a wee sleep
Inside my slipper.
Slippers. What the hell was I thinking?

We said farewell in the Drovers.
A good lunch,
A self-inflating mattress
And a fiver
Were proffered and accepted.
I proceeded alone and
Took my shredded feet to Crianlarich.

On the bridge over the single-track railway
I waved at the southbound driver,
Who of course waved back and sounded the horn.
Mein neuer Freund aus Stuttgart,
Er war erstaunt.
This would never happen in Germany.
I was like a magician to him
And swelled with cultural pride.

Next the heathery shoulder past Bridge of Orchy,
And a brisk skirting of Rannoch Moor in fair weather,
To the island in the river in the
Illustrious presence of Buachaille Etive Mòr.

A surplus of time no boon in Kinlochleven
For one too young and shy for the Antler Bar.
So I read every single word of the Aluminium Story,
Where it wasnae raining,
Twice.
As for my early evening meal,
More than twenty years on, it remains
           the worst haggis supper I've ever had.
I can still see the raindrops landing on the
Nasty thick crunchy batter,
Rivulets flowing down onto the
Biscuit-hard chips.

It was a difficult spot.
The soil was no more than one inch thick.
Shallow peg anchorage
Made for a lengthy, rain-drenched
Midge-tormented experience.
The tent finally assembled,
I crawled in, exhausted,
The stupidly heavy, soaking rucksack needed moved.
I decided to shift it across to the other side of the tent
So I lay down, embraced it to my chest
Like a somewhat smaller lover,
Rolled over to my left,
Heaving the sodden weighty bag over myself.
My glasses crunched uncomfortably
Beneath the small of my back.

As the rain entered its thirtieth consecutive hour
In a small clearing in Nevis Forest.
Box of matches soaked through,
Despite my best efforts with the plastic bags.
Fork in one hand,
Cold tin of Heinz Spaghetti Bolognese in the other,
I ate.

Down in the glen,
A truly fabulous hot chocolate waited for me,
And another new German pal.

Like the smell of abandoned butter,
Or perhaps salt and vinegar crisps
Too many months in the bag,
My trousers whistled an angry tune,
Keeping clear the seats around me
On the Fort William to Glasgow train.
I stopped off to see him on my way home, rang the doorbell,
And pushed my self-repaired spectacles back up my nose.
The door opened. He looked at me.
The Elastoplast holding my glasses together
Gave way,
Leaving one lens dangling,
Swinging from side to side in front of my face.
He laughed loud and long
As well he might.

THE MORNING OF IAN ROUGVIE

The Minister of State for Badness and Terrifying Events, Mr Ian Rougvie, awoke in the Second Glasgow Hilton. He had booked himself in there the previous night, that is to say it had not been his PA who had made the arrangements. Rougvie was a forgiving man, and he had given Hatty the whole week off to help her recover from the injuries she had incurred two days previously following her near-self-immolation.

That is to say, she had set fire to her own head, following her enthusiastically literal interpretation of one of Rougvie's own Government Bills.

Rougvie had had something of a "rough ride" from the hacks and the Socialist Labour Party of Caledonia members there at yesterday's press conference, but the motion had been passed by the party membership the previous day that would enable him to lodge his short bill at Holyrood to secure in statute Glasgow's inaugural Fanning the Flames of Sectarianism Festival.

During his sleepingness there in that plush room on the sixteenth floor (most of the other rooms being occupied by balaclava-clad teenage French terrorists on an undercover exchange visit to their twin cell, the Renfrew Pyrotechnic Disruption Front), he had a dream. It involved an agreeable stroll in a North American metropolis, in which the skyscrapers were sheathed with gigantic rubber prophylactics. Rougvie's dream persona started running around a city park (Central Park? not sure), growing more and more anxious and confused at the situation. The great big things were flapping around worryingly in the increasingly strong wind.

Back in the hotel, Rougvie's door was chapped upon, that is to say someone was knocking on it. It was the maid, with Rougvie's breakfast room service. She greeted him with "Ya fuckin snotty-faced bastard!

Couldnae fuckin satisfy a blow-up doll!"

"Thanks for that," Rougvie replied, "ya smelly peat-munchin hoor!" He gave her the obligatory 10 per cent tip, that is to say he offered her a one euro coin, which she snatched, before sucking phlegm into the back of her mouth and spitting heavily on his dressing gown.

The breakfast was delicious. Rougvie took a piece of hotel notepaper, wrote "thanks" on it in biro, masturbated on it and put it on the plate upon which his egg, beans and square sausage had been served. He left the tray out in the corridor, just outside his door. However, he realised that the tray had come to rest on an object, that is to say it did not lie flat when he came to put it down on the carpet of the corridor. He shifted the tray along some to see what it was that was underneath.

It was a big mousetrap. In a split-second the metal snare snapped onto his hand, breaking his thumb.

This required surgery, which would no doubt retard his day's agenda. That was unfortunate. It was all so frustrating, and it made him think once again about his proposals to the First Minister to decriminalise being nasty in hospitals. Surely worth a shot, especially after his proposals for the new group stabbing regulations had come so close to being introduced.

Rougvie was worried. The police were bound to catch up with him in the next day or two. He had been rude to a newspaper seller the other morning and had aimed a kick at her shins, having failed to notice her orange Infirmity badge. That is to say, he had broken the law by failing to restrain his abuse on that occasion to the verbals, flicking the v and such. There were plenty of witnesses. Don't injure the already injured – that was the well-established, humane law of the land. The press would be all over him sooner or later. He might have to resign. That would be most unfortunate indeed.

The rest of the Cabinet had been forgiving about most things, but maybe this personal scandal would be more of a challenge. It was quite a different job explaining away, for example, the chronic nurse shortage, which was a result of the 30,000% increase in the number of hospitals – a necessity under Rougvie's new social policy. There were now at least two clinics on the average street in Glasgow, Edinburgh, Aberdeen and Dundee, and there were few Highland villages left without at least a sub-accident and emergency unit – which were pretty popular, as they often had breakfast rolls, tea and coffee available, as well as brochures and things for tourists. There was full employment although, admittedly, the tax burden was now rather beefy.

Rougvie made his way downstairs. He clocked a porter carrying bags down the stairs from the seventeenth floor – the staff were not allowed to use the elevators. Following a moment's thought, he surprised the porter, that is to say he deftly turned and punched him very hard in the stomach. The porter dropped the suitcases and took a few seconds to recover himself. After regaining his balance, the porter faced Rougvie, gaped in recognition of this very important Government minister, and after still more of a pause, punched him on the side of the face. Rougvie slumped to one side. The porter said "sorry".

Rougvie, enraged at the apology, bellowed, "Do you know who I am, boy?" The porter indicated his next apology silently, that is to say he made his mouth go long and looked down at the ground, but then, inspired, cracked Rougvie's chin with his elbow. "Fuckin hell," moaned Rougvie. "Ah must've bitten hauf ma fuckin tongue aff."

The bleeding was so profuse that he would have to visit the hotel hospital immediately, before attempting any official business. At least he had already taken advantage of room service: you never want to go to hospital in the morning without breakfast, especially not on a Friday.

He paged the junior minister for acute health monitoring to say he would now be late for their Perth meeting, and to add that she was a ratbag with a despicable, malodorous husband.

This coming Sunday, being the first of the month, was being gentle and paying compliments day. Perhaps it would be all right, and perhaps the good people of Scotland, walking, hobbling and wheelchairing to church with all their monstrous scars and assorted crippling injuries, would be able to enjoy a restful day.

aphorisms and musings (iii)

125. The excitement that one enjoys by cleaning out one's ears with cotton buds upon going to bed having already turned the light out, leaving the cotton buds on one's bedside table and waiting until the morning light before inspecting their appearance must surely rank only a little below that of undersea discovery.

126. The exterior of Dofos pet shop is very solid indeed. Never run full tilt into it.

127. The goodness of the left.

128. The less dirigiste your God, the less your faith will be tested.

129. The life experiences of little children make me weep.

130. The mathematics of the radioactive half-life apply in exactly the same way to the frequency with which you discover your ex-girlfriend's hairs in your flat after she's moved out.

131. The more one reads about the horrific customs of the ancient Romans, the better one understands why they insisted on crucifying top good guy Jesus for those threateningly conciliatory ideas of his.

132. The more one understands human nature, the more one's moans and complaints become tactical.

133. The most difficult sort of strength to muster in yourself is the strength that you need in order to protect your own weakness.

134. The most problematic generation gap can be zero.

135. The mystery of our existence is guaranteed to remain a mystery if you choose to frame your thoughts about it using unanswerable questions.

136. The name for the necessary compromise of one's ideals is Politics.

137. The only laws you actually have to follow are those that have not been made up by people.

138. The original mistake swells in size if it is repeated.

139. The purpose of most decisions is to stave off insecurity.

140. The question is, of course: *does* push come to shove?

141. The rule of law is only ever partial. Its extent depends on culture, contentment, material comfort, enforcement and levels of sanity and education among the general populace, among other factors.

142. The tears and snotters of women will eventually penetrate through the shoulder and seep into the hearts of men. It is a pity that these hearts are so often made of fibreboard.

143. The voices of the future are silent.

144. The weather is always twice as mysterious and menacing before you leave the house in the morning.

145. The worst symptom of love-blindness among women is faith in man; the worst symptom of love-blindness among men is faith in man.

146. The wound might be so deep that only the knife will cure you.

147. *Theoretically*, the atheist's world has fewer commonly agreed rules and therefore contains more of a risk of anarchy and terror.

148. There are big nations with a superiority complex; there are small nations with an inferiority complex; and there is Belgium.

149. There are only two possible ways to be on your own: as if no-one is anywhere near or as if someone might be there soon.

150. There are people who will often say "99.999 per cent of the time" when they actually mean about 94 per cent of the time at most. Do not trust such people.

151. There is no correlation between importance and complexity.

152. There is so much to enjoy about England.

153. There is such a thing as political correctness, and there is such a thing as political correctness gone mad. If your political leanings are to the left, you will understand that political correctness means a conscious avoidance of needlessly discriminatory words and actions, especially insulting or unpleasant ones. If your political leanings are to the right, you might feel that political correctness *is* mad, and that largely explains why you keep saying "It's political correctness gone mad."

154. There will still be spoons in the year 2200, albeit fewer per head of population.

155. Third, fourth, fifth… NOT reverse next.

156. "This always happens" is a false claim, a specious attempt to highlight the exceptionally inconvenient while trying to wipe countless everyday events and phenomena from history. You do not pull the wool over my eyes, oh no.

157. This Itchycoo Park place. I'm starting to suspect it's actually some sort of *metaphor*.

158. Those who die virgins will have had to deal with sex more.

159. To view others' views as wrong, we should first take account of the lens that is our conditioning.

160. Truth is a multifaceted clod.

161. Truth is a purely linguistic construct.

162. We are all naked and vulnerable, and our own desperate gossip has fooled us into thinking that somewhere is a gown to cover and warm us, called Meaning.

163. What is really important in the world? Probably the things that make you cry.

164. What we yearn for in our imagination is intolerable in reality.

165. When one arrives at a new place of employment, should one learn the rules, the culture or the sub-culture first?

166. When talking to yourself, even if you are completely alone, you must correct any factual or grammatical mistakes you make. Otherwise, you will be guilty of self-deception.

167. When you really feel you want to arse a whole bottle of whisky, don't.

168. When you're sitting in a train, trying to put down some thoughts in the form of aphorisms, you might get distracted by the fellow passenger's mobile phone conversation, which is punctuated with some regularity by the phrases, "Aye aye, bud," and "Okey-coke." However, you are tickled by this, so you don't complain.

169. Wisdom is revealed to others through the habitual voicing of correct impressions.

170. Wisdom you will accumulate as you get older; you may show compassion, however, at any age.

171. With gastronomy comes death.

172. "Yes" and "No": each carries its own treachery.

172B: Yesterday I sicked a mixture of carbonara and tiramisu out my nose. It was worth it, though.

173. Yon loon wearin a baseball hat. Says
PARIS
FRANCE
Aabody fuckin kens Paris is in fuckin France.

174. You are not alone in preferring softer crisps.

175. You can't just keep moping around the flat, spending the whole time wishing you were more of a decisive man of action, like a Patrick McGoohan character. Just go out for a walk or something.

176. You can't talk about your life using the expression "Oh, just the same old same old" if you're under 35.

177. You know when you've really lost your self-respect when someone else has to tell you.

178. You look down the pan, and you abhor and fear the skid mark.

179. You may absorb either twice or half the amount of the love and kindness that is bestowed upon you. It depends whether your soul is convex or concave.

180. You may think that other people confuse you a lot; don't forget how easily you can confuse them.

181. You might feel alienated by the faceless corporate machine that oppresses you, but of course it's really just a collection of other frightened human beings.

182. You should consider the potential advantage you may hold if your enemy is squeamish about eating quiche.

183. You will be respected, Thompson, when people stop calling you 'Thompo' and start calling you 'Raging-Beast' or 'Mad-Dog'.

184. You're an adult once you start smelling like one.

CARELESSNESS

I woke up with the most massive feet.

I know what you're thinking. Swollen feet can be so uncomfortable –
Poor thing! Oh dear Swollen feet Not nice etc. etc.

Or alternatively, you might be thinking what I first thought when I
woke up. Which was that I must have become a character in one of those
peculiar Russian short stories I got for Christmas. Although in this instance
my feet had not (yet) gone off and started parading about, leading a life
(lives) of their own etc. etc.

Leaving me with stumps.

Anyway.

But what they had done was grown to an extreme size. That's what
you need to understand. They'd doubled. Twice as big, they were.

My wife, with her little bird-like feet, was immediately resentful.
Jealous, is what I mean.

I would have been annoyed, annoyed or embarrassed, to be seen at
such a time by my twenty-year-old son Bob (or Rab, as he is known to the
world outside the house – he seems convinced that 'Bob' makes him out
to be some sort of drooling imbecile, which I have to say is a matter of
something like regret or sadness on my part, or just pure irritation, but he
wasn't likely to be getting up before midday in all likelihood), or by my
daughter, Tina, (possibly *Christina* when introducing herself to boys, or
men, shudder, in nightclubs, in Barcelona, where she was for five days,
and nights, see shudder above.

Close brackets.

Getting on with it, and rolling into the present tense for the moment,
as per some seemingly deft if accidental key change:

So here's what. I go out, and straight away I'm frightening the kids I pass on the pavement, so I'm constantly saying sorry. Shoes have become useless to me now, so I've had to fashion some coverings out of cardboard and taped-up bin bags for going along the pavements. Like some horrible street baffies that look very wrong. Walking is really pretty sore.

The GP is apologetic, says there must have been some mix-up. How has this happened? etc. etc. I'm asking, but trying to be civil.

Well, it's a kind of experiment, I'm told. Really? It sort of came about in a discussion between me and Dr Rashid, she says. It was an idea that went a wee bit wrong, or wasn't supposed to happen to people in my cohort, whatever she means by that.

When I first went in (just slightly before, so past tense now, okay?) I thought I ought to get straight to the nub, so I just pointed at my feet, which looked like plasticine when you've mixed all the colours up into a sickening grey-brown, and I said What do you call this?

Ah. I'm truly sorry etc. etc.

But there isn't anything you can do about it? Is that what you're saying? What are you playing at? etc. Me, and also my wife, we're at our wits' end, sort of thing.

Tense pause.

The doctor's heart-breaking silence is eventually broken by an Of course there's something you can do, smiling. You'd hardly want your feet to stay like that permanently, would you!!

Yeah.

So, Doctor prescribes me a wooden mallet, and some little pills made by FlaxySpitClutch and tells us the only other ingredient needed at home is table salt.

Like a *larder item*, I'm thinking.

"Is that okay?"

We nod.

They were normal size again by about a month later, which frankly was a much better outcome than I had feared i.e. massive feet until time of death, although the pain and blistering and flappy bits of skin weren't very nice.

And my wife was saying "Why not book a follow-up appointment? See if you can't find out what it was all about, with your feet?" and I wasn't sure that would help or lead to anything, but I went along to the doctor's after another week or so, and I wasn't sure at first if it was my GP I saw coming out the building just as I was approaching, as she had a big John Lewis bag covering her now ginormous head, with holes cut out for the eyes, and when she passed me, because I'd stopped on the pavement, staring, she seemed a bit distressed, but she recognised me, and it was her right enough, and said she couldn't see me that day, and she was once again apologetic.

MY BELGIAN MUZHIK

Another air mail letter arrived on an Aberdour doormat.

"Dear Mum,

Hope Dad's feelin better.

What a weekend this is turnin oot tae be! Ah wis totally feart yesterday when Karen and Paul made us go tae Gorky Park. This German rollercoaster wis pure mental – wouldnae have trusted the thing at all if it had been Russian-built, eh!"

And, some five weeks afterwards, a daughter in Moscow tore open an envelope – because she always tore open envelopes – to find out what her mother had to say this time. Most of it was just chat, with a small proportion of useless advice and a further small proportion of useful advice, all in the same tight curls of blue biro. Laura had only just rounded the post-adolescent corner of being able to consider advice at all rationally, and it still made her smart to understand and agree with the odd maternal word of wisdom.

Mum's letter had only reached the second paragraph before it stung. "I do wish you wouldn't write like that," it went. "I don't know why you have to write like that, given your education."

"And you can even write in the Russian as well!" it chipped in, two paragraphs further down. It obviously hadn't left her system the first time, so she had to get her pen all busy about it again down the bottom of the first page. Just to piss her off.

The rest was mainly along the lines of "don't trust boys after dark," or some such theory. She wasn't far off the mark there. Amazing, but true: with very few exceptions, the boys that stayed in the student hostel (Russians, English, Scots, Czechs, Yanks and representatives of all three Low Countries) were tossers of the first order.

That Dmitri – "Dinnae start" she would say every time her roommate Helen mentioned his name – had given her such a hard time at Karen's birthday *vecherinka* for daring to mix her vodka with tonic, and kept telling her to switch to the OJ instead. "Aye," she had thought on more than one occasion, "Ye can stick yer orange *sok* where the sun dinnae shine." When she had tried to express the same in Russian, Dmitri had replied with words that she couldn't understand.

But then there was her current intrigue.

1: Chris, Felixstowe, Suffolk. After me. Nice face, incl. big jaw (good sign). Good at colloq. Russ. Proved willing to skive translation class for coffee in funny mafia-run caff. Interests: beer; otherwise unknown.

2: Maurice, smwhr nr. Brussels. Shy – otherwise, would be after me. Wee face and silly glasses, but incred. bod. Good at colloq. Russ. Dedicated attender, but bought me drinks down the *Vopros* once without letting me buy him back any (such stupidity acceptable). Interests: squash, skiing. Likely vg in bed. Gd eye cont.

3: Dmitri, Khimki, nr. Moscow. Juist leave me alane, Mitya, eh!

Probably best not to go into those details in correspondence, as Mum would only give her opinion about what was right or sensible – which of course had nothing to do with reality.

Laura took a grainy piece of A4 from the pad she'd bought in the French supermarket – and bloody expensive it had been as well.

"Dear mum," blah blah blah.

"Could be a Belgian boy or even a nice English chap – yes, such things are possible.

...They cleaned the halls for cockroaches last week so I haven't seen any more in the kitchen."

She realised what a stupid idea it had been to have told her about that in the first place two letters ago – Mum had almost got on the phone to the uni back hame. Shouldnae have mentioned them. What the hell did she expect? Cockroaches everywhere here.

"Will give you another call from the international phone place up the road shortly after you get this."

That was meant to be "efter youse get this" or something, but she saw no reason to keep on at it.

One Thursday night, they all went out. They took the metro, even though it felt a bit silly them going just one stop. But it had been none other than Maurice Overberghe who had pointed out how long it would take them to get there on foot – 30 minutes, and that would be Forrest-Gumping it.

This would be her fourth visit to the *Drugoi Vopros* – the Other

Question, the foreignish bar with the friendly inside and the dubious, heavily guarded outside. And exclusively Pripps 1828 on tap, for some funny reason.

Anyway, Laura's drinking companions that night were Paul, Helen, Ruraidh and Volodya, Dmitri's more sensible pal, a pale, quiet guy with a nice slow voice who lived in the halls because he was from Krasnoyarsk. And Maurice.

"You want to stay there late tonight?" Maurice asked as they stepped off the up escalator in the quiet marble-floored metro station. He had phrased his question perfectly as far as meaning went, but it still wasn't quite right stylistically. The translator in Laura made her rephrase it in her head, and it became "Youse oan fir a late yin the night?"

"I never plan to stay out late, Maurice, never plan to," she answered, fixing his eyes with hers through the fringe of her hair, feeling familiar and quite adult towards him, thinking about how it might look to him – hoping how it might look to him – giving him that coy sidelong glance, conscious of her ear stud sparkling and her neat blond highlights shading half her eye.

She had a half; he had a pint. The western beer, albeit Scandiwegian and until recently unfamiliar, made her and everyone else from the other side of Bohemia feel more at home and confident. Someone with a pony tail and stubble had a guitar hanging between his arms. Songs composed in Britain in the 60s had been chic here for ages and there was no sign of any let-up, unfortunately. She had to get terribly defensive to Dmitri once about her not being able to name more than six Beatles songs, even claiming that wasn't all that bad. In fact, Laura had successfully turned the tables on him, and D was now often to be heard trying out numbers from the "This is the Story" album she'd lent him on cassette: "To meik sure mai vords on your Syexon ears don't greit."

After two beers, Maurice got her alone at a table.

And after four days, he got her alone up on Gorky Park's massive Ferris wheel.

Four days. It felt like weeks. In a good way, of course.

But as good as his company was, she now just wanted him to burst into her. Not in a bodily or physical sense as such – although why not? – but just... They'd seen each other three times now, and it really was high time for it.

She couldn't tell if it was him that was holding back or if it was actually her. Mibbe baith, she speculated. They were both wanting to latch onto each other, certainly, but despite all their concentrated time together, nothing much was actually happening for some reason. And that was despite every tree all around them exploding in green.

He had been so cool. What had he done that was so amazing? Stood next to her in a certain way, spoken in a certain tone and at a certain volume, not shaven for just the right length of time, worn the right jeans, known when she wanted to eat, introduced her to a new cocktail? All incidental. He was young, he had engaging eyes. And he *was* amazing, she could sense it. The fact was, in the space of just a few days, he had taken some sort of benevolent, undefined ownership of her.

Over those four days since they had first squashed their mouths together down the *Vopros*, things had seemed to move really fast, but without getting very far on paper, as it were. He had got a hold of her, focused on her, yes – but he hadn't quite *burst* yet. So, none of the bed thing or anything.

Emotionally, though, there was already attachment. Sealed. It had started in earnest. Definitely.

They hardly knew each other. Whirlwind, but.

"Dear mum.

Things have been moving quickly, all right.

...giving us more translation work to do again, and the topics are getting a bit weird.

...article about some daft woman growing prize vegetables, which we've got to translate into Russian.

...Maurice. He's got light brown hair, blue eyes and he's very polite. You'd probably want him for yourself! He also speaks Dutch and German and some Spanish too, and he..."

And so on.

She took Maurice a mug of Dutch herbal tea and set it down on the table. Helen was away for the day.

She winced at the oily surface of the beverage. It was like the traces of petrol on the forecourt at that big filling station at Dalgety Bay, which she had a twinge of homesickness for, for some daft reason. It was in *The Moscow Times* she'd read about all the manure and muck you got in the tapwater in the spring.

"Chemicals," she remarked.

"Aye, I ken," he replied, very nearly getting her accent right.

She sat on his knee, just like she'd done at the party they had been to along the corridor a couple of days back. She turned towards the fruit bowl, reached over and coaxed him to take a bite of apple.

"Symbolic, eh?" she whispered. Something flashed over the surface of his face in response to that, but she couldn't read it. She got up, turned round again and sat across him, fixing herself in his eyes, although he kept looking away and staring into space.

"Dear Mum,
…found a new shop near the city centre that sells all sorts of stuff for cooking and storing cutlery and things.

...never know with the old grannies selling all sorts of stuff in the underpasses. Most of them are all right, though, and it seems to be normal to do lots of your shopping there.

...and yes, it's still going great. It's a really nice thought and a comfort having somebody with me to share this term."

"That's me finished in the shower, eh."
"Righto," replied Helen.

It was as she was towelling herself off, that Tuesday morning before consecutive interpreting class at 10.30, that Laura was first aware of the emotional tick in her head. What if he wasn't ever going to *burst*? What if she was waiting for him to burst, but he just wasn't going to? All sorts of peripheral thoughts were crowding round her brain too, but that was the only one that articulated itself into words. With almost telepathic insensitivity, Helen asked, "Seeing your gorgeous man today?"

"Of course," snapped her roommate.

She's had a tick, thought Helen. He's only gone and given her the tick. She went back through into her room to get her things ready, shaking her head and sighing in sympathy.

Laura made a hot chocolate after they'd all come back from the ballet, using the last of the Cadbury's sachets she'd brought from home. There was Maurice, next to her all the time at parties or out in restaurants or just there at the theatre. Touching her leg. Saying stuff. And?

She picked up the pad from the bed, with its bizarre diamond-shaped hole in the sheet that all the beds here seemed to have.

"Dear Mum," she wrote, and hesitated. There he was. Overberghe. And there was his body and his politeness and his intelligence, but…

Tick, tick, tick.

She tutted and shook her head.

"I got your letter yesterday. Thanks. Glad to hear Uncle Philip thought it best to rush back. Probably the best thing – sounded like an absolute nightmare with his asthma.

Everything's fine hear."

She stopped, astonished. She showed Helen, who chuckled and told her it was a good sign – she must be learning too much Russian if the

English was getting squeezed out of her head.

"Here," she wrote over it, in heavier ink. "Have been going out with Maurice for 12 or 13 days only, but it feels like ages. I mean in a good way! We've been across the river to Gorky Park loads of times, and he got me out of a real scrape when these Russian teenagers tried to sell us marijuana."

She looked out the window and listened to the springtime noises outside as she ripped the paper up into small strips. She gathered it up and tried to reassemble it into a ball, but it just flaked apart again. Half an hour later, she produced an alternative account of events with no drug dealers.

The party in room 504 was dire. Lucy, from North Carolina, was in a wild mood, and she had even told the *kommandantka* of the hostel where to go when she'd asked them to turn the music down. Lucy was high on champagne; the middle-aged lady was usually fearsome but, incredibly, she disappeared on this occasion with nothing more than "Enjoy yourselves then, but more quietly, please, *rebyata*."

For some reason Maurice was late. Which made Laura anxious – and anxiously she flirted with Chris, who was sitting closer and closer and was quite probably about to start pawing her, like a half-sedated Labrador.

Maurice turned up. He looked and nodded at everyone. "Hi," he said to Lucy, Darren, Frank, Chris, Yelena, Sergei, Anton and Emma. And finally, finally, *finally* Laura.

Well piss off then, she juddered inside.

Maurice's arm couldn't be wrapped any more tightly round her. His thighs and the bulge in his trousers and his burgeoning six-pack and his eyes and his niceness couldn't be any more real. They were both gazing uninterestedly into the middle of the room, not quite focusing on the half-Russian, half-English flirting and nonsense and arguments about house music and John Lennon.

He got up and walked over to the toilet, looking back at her and warming her up with the glow of a smile.

Why don't you just burst, Maurice? Just burst all over me and stop holding back.

"Hey, honey! What's up?"

She had been speaking out loud, as it turned out. She looked nervously at Emma, who was from somewhere near Orlando and was blearily communicating concern, sitting down next to her. She shrugged. Emma seemed to understand, but moved away again, trying once more to outmanoeuvre Lucy for the goal of the gorgeous Sergei. Laura spoke to her Soviet Champagne in its plastic cup, and told it that it would be the last one.

He came back out of the toilet and looked at Emma, not her. Laura's head popped somewhere on the inside. She glanced again at the sticky fizzy liquid, and poured it into the plant pot. Aye, this would be the last one, she told herself – not because she necessarily meant it, but because saying it seemed like some sort of progress. And it would be the last time anyone would clunkingly say "Let's hope this works," to her in some rip-off foreign Moscow bar, with a seductive wink, too much aftershave and…

The room swam.

"Dear Mum"

There were so many tears on the letter that she had had to write it all out again. All of it. Her handwriting was much neater and the letter was more evenly folded the second time. But she hardly changed a word. As such.

"Thanks for your letter. I know you're looking forward to meeting Maurice already. I know you'd like him. A bit quiet but you…"

She muttered in Russian under her breath, wiping the end of her hair away from her red eyes.

"…ken they Belgians, eh. No a loud nationality.

…Anyway, everything's going fine with Maurice. I thought you sounded keen in your last letter. There's no need to ask about him more than once per page, though!"

She furrowed her brow, and willed herself to cry.

"We get on well together at uni too, and…"

This was dire.

"…makes me laugh a lot."

Was there anything more pointless? Really, was there anything to all this?

"Ah should be sittin here knowin that Ah belong tae somebody," she wrote on a new bit of paper, *"but Ah dinnae ken that."* Laura had decided she could write a letter to herself, too. This would say different things, though.

"It's no the language barrier that's the problem. He juist connects wi an idea o me, an no really wi the real me."

"His English is perfect but not, if you know what I mean. He uses all the right words and expressions, but just not the same ones that we would necessarily use in the same situation."

"It's like Ah cannae see his emotions. An whit does he care aboot mines? Ah've put them intae this game ay his, an they're aa oan display. Dis eh huv any hissel? Wid Ah care aboot his proablems? Ah dinnae even ken, eh."

"If I can persuade him to come to Scotland sometime…"

Helen came in the door with some shopping, rushing towards the out-of-breath gulping of Laura's sobs, applying the sympathy and understanding of a half-foreigner, half-compatriot. Through the wash of salt water and over the mothering horizon of Helen's shoulder, Laura reread the last line and imagined what it would be like if it were in a movie: some candle would suddenly go out or her biro would explode ink or some fucking thing. That's what it felt like should happen.

And as she swam away into her daydreams, held tightly by Helen's arms (she was a dozy wee bisom fae Hampshire, but she was still a guid friend, sister or somethin) she thought of home. Hame? Even Heathrow would do at the minute – it was close enough to that Dalgety Bay petrol station.

And as she yearned for its wide selection of crisps and warm-upable snacks and its ice lollies, she wondered what she would miss about here? Not being able to keep a straight face ordering a Vispa or a Tvix from a street kiosk whenever Ruraidh was around? The nice man with the bus-driver moustache who took the grammar class? The lovely creamy mashed potatoes in the otherwise rank *stolovaya*? The ice cream, no doubt – eating that lovely rock-hard ice cream out on the street in sub-zero temperatures. She'd miss that.

And she'd miss the first few precious days of Maurice.

"Okay?" Helen's voice broke through her tearful suds.

Tick.

"Yeah," smiled Laura. She had thought of the first line after the "Dear Mum" of her next letter. It would start confidently. "Some less good news to begin with, I'm afraid."

THE HOT SWEET

Once again, it's going to be tight. The deadline is in 29 minutes; it would take about 40 minutes to see enough of the show and type the thing up if I was actually going to do this properly.

If I'm going to avoid Spaggert getting really cross and phoning me up, I'll need to get the piece finished and sent in no more than 35 minutes, realistically – one must eventually settle on such compromises. Aye, I've trained myself to act cool when he gives me any hassle but, deep down, Spaggert getting really cross on the phone is one of the few things in life that still makes me scared.

No, that doesn't do it justice. See scared? See five years old and a gigantic dog coming arfing towards you with dinosaur-size saliva trails swinging? See being an 18-year-old trainee with the Clydesdale Bank and getting a hold-up to deal with just after your first ever coffee break? See nodding off on the flight to Mallorca and hearing the sirens and "Brace positions! Brace positions!"? See giving the Enterprise Minister a tour round the building on his official visit and he passes out through food poisoning after a dodgy canteen fish and asparagus wrap that you'd spent ages persuading him to have?

Aye, and that reminds me. I've got to go back and have lunch with Calum Clewstrie today. Old Clewsters has some pretty brainy ideas for the marketing division in Warsaw, and he reckons they can "be proactively rolled out across the wider zone going forward," to use the vacuous pseudo-managerial lingo that even he now feels obliged to come out with. And given that I am Euro East Coordinator these days, I am the very it-person for him to have lunch with.

But moonlighting always comes first. 40 minutes or so to kick off my lunch break, and a cheeky wee credit for €150 in the bank account by the following day. Then, usually, fifteen minutes to actually eat my lunch – unless of course it's a working lunch like today.

"Medic in a Spin" came to our screens last night on the back of a mercifully short-lived set of trailers deluging us with promises of the well-moisturised chests and ham acting to come. I prepared myslef ARSE *myself for some pretty low-risk camera work, low-cut costumes on the shiny-bodied, doe-eyed actresses and low-vocabulary exchanges of platitudes by flustered medical men and womemm* N, YOU FUCKER *women who, in the best televisual tradition, somehow never actually speak over each other while interrupting.*

Quite apart from being stubbornly unfunny, "Medic in a Spin" promises to be a serial uncomplicated by excess directorial ambition. Even in this first episoefa JESUS *episode, the sluttish female leads ape a shamelessly repetitive script that helps the programme slot nicely into the dirty housewives section of this year's tired offering of superformulaic melodramaporn.*

In case readers are not entirely Fred Astaire of the extent of this reviewer's feelings about "Medic", let me just conclude by saying that I hate to imagine the arse-asphyxiating numbness I might feel should a further abhorrent slimy crap-gush excrescence of cod-awful pseudo-medi drip-drip storytelling jism, namely episode two, pass before my eyes.

Viewers, my lovelies, consider whether your brain is made of faeces. If so, carry on watching "Medic in a Spin". You never lisgened HITTING THE RIGHT KEYS WOULD BE NICE, DICKFACE *listened to me before, so why start now and curtail your scabby television-watching habit, you junkie trash of the small screen, and deprive yourself of the only turds of pleasure you ever get?*

I mail it to Spaggert a few minutes early. I know the pig-faced tyrant will be sitting attentively at his screen and, to my non-surprise, I see his **Recipient has read your mail** message popping up with a prickish beep after less than five seconds. A reply will be with me, probably, in another three minutes tops, so I take the opportunity to put my necky back on and finish my coffee. I check my carpass and see I've only got another 20 lowtax miles left on my account this month, arsing bastardfuck of a situation as that is.

1 minute 55 seconds have passed without reply. Ah – something I must do: I'll be back in Gdansk first thing next week and I want a sexy Baltic haircut offof Kat. I phone her number.

"Hi, it's me. Chciałabym zamówić wizytę... Tak. How you doing, Kat? No, no. What? Nie rozumiem… Poniedziałek. Yes. Ten o'clock. Yes, ten, that's right. I chciałabym pasemek... Is that right? Tak. Woah, wait a minute. Nie, nie, nie! That was a joke. No, I don't want highlights. No. No pasemka, thank you... Wie bitte? Einen Messerschnitt. No, and no more Rauchkäse this time, okay? Yeah, yeah. See you then. Do zobaczenia, sweetheart – Tschüss."

What a fucking disaster of a phone call. Total crossed wires there. I probably got most of that wrong. I'll end up with a razorblade sandwich for lunch and getting a beard trim with a sharpened slice of fucking cheese.

Ah! Pop goes the reply.

A bit harsh, Steve. Don't make me edit so much next time. Go back to work.

I think about that for a bit and decide it's pretty glowing. I breathe easy.

Back down the road, I reach the drones' cafeteria, put my plastic cup under that nozzle and fire some water into it. Glug glug glug. He's not here. So I have another cup. And another one, and another, over and over again – I might end up drowning myself if he doesn't get here soon.

I start to feel almost blootered on the water, but then CC turns up, 11 minutes late and terribly apologetic. We both choose the duck paste and coriander filo thing. It is slightly dry.

"So, if you had the same system at Prague II, for example, you'd get far more balanced commission between the country agents and less cross-referencing between departments."

"And less internal invoicing," I suggest.

"Exactly," replies Clewsters, his eyes pulsing with eagerness.

"Yeah, well, I don't see any reason for that not to work as long as it's introduced across the board for the new financial year."

"Well, we're doing shadow accounts for the whole of the Poland group for this year. Audit say yes and we can roll it out to everywhere else next year."

"Very good, Calum." I nod. This is Clewsters at his best, and he should certainly get the credit for it. "If you get go-ahead from level B, you could fire off a big article for *Bulletin East* two months from now, say – and then you could be gunning for my job," I smile with the right-hand half of my mouth.

Clewstrie nods with a cheerful blend of modesty and excitement. Then an altogether different face appears – a familiar expression of unsatisfied desire. Surely, with no time left in my already stretched lunch hour, surely Clewstrie is not going to make us have a hot sweet.

"I'm just going to see what's for pudding, Steve."

"Sure." I can't express more than those four letters of stolid acknowledgement as reaction. In the circumstances I have to keep him company for as long as he wants to spin out his lunch – that much is only common courtesy, but it's a bit of a palaver. People at our level of middle management don't do pudding; that's really the preserve of the top brass, or of people much lower down who have not yet learned how to value their time. Clewstrie's appetite is legendary, however, as is its illogical juxtaposition against his trim frame. His metabolism runs on scramjets, the rest of us have concluded. Without these puddings, he would undoubtedly flake out every time he went to the gym.

He comes back with a school-dinner throwback third course – a lump of thing in a pond of yellow custard. "What's that?" I ask.

"Banana fritter," he replies. He spoons a little custard to his lips. "It's not very hot," he reports. "I'll take it back and get another."

Oh god. "Absolutely," I say, and wag my hand in the direction of the counter in reluctant encouragement.

My mind is blank as Calum strides purposefully towards the kitchen staff, pudding bowl resolutely clutched, and I check my diary to see when I'm on interview panel. Three, then four. Easy afternoon.

He returns and smiles, holding a bowl with thing ("fritter") and custard as before. However, his smile soon dissipates.

"It's the same one. They just put it in the microwave."

"Well," I reply, "surely that's what they would…"

"It's the same one. I asked for a new one. This is just the same one. Look. The custard's all…"

It is indeed rather thin – only a short distance from being yellow milk. It looks like he's going to take it back again. Incredible.

"And look at this!" he adds, brandishing his spoon and attacking the layer of syrup over the spongey interior. Tap tap tap. "It's hard!"

"Well…"

"It's hard. They've just put it in the microwave. It's the same one."

I put my head in my hands and consider how this pudding episode is postponing the start of my afternoon activities – I actually have a lot of mails to write to various movers and shakers in Warsaw and LA in particular, and I also have a wife's birthday to think about.

And he's off. I shake my head and glance knowingly at Madeleine Lees and Ian Rush (no relation to the 1980s soccer legend) at the next table, but they are unaware of the pudding business unfolding before me, being locked in conversation about the French licensing agreement that went pear-shaped – another Marseille office cock-up – and have no idea why I'm staring at them. I mouth "Tell you later" at them and they nod confusedly.

Calum returns in a pretty ratty mood, plonking his bowl down like a bad audit. "I can't believe it. Look at the custard. Look at it!" I look at it. It is mottled. White bits have appeared. I form the opinion that they've put it back in the microwave for a second time. However, the contours of the fritter are unmistakably different.

"That's a new bit," concedes Clewstrie, prodding at a spongey outcrop, "but I reckon that's just the old one," he contends, pointing to the main corpus of banana thing. On reflection, I agree. He scoops the custard and soft parts into his mouth and says, "It is hotter."

"Good," I offer.

The syrupy part is evidently a bit more pliable now. Clewstrie succeeds in getting a bit of it to separate from the main banana island, takes it into his mouth and, for the first time I have seen today, chews in a satisfied way. I have almost forgotten about the coffee I have procured for myself and, with the idiotic surprise one experiences when remembering something that one has already done for oneself, I take the cup, phooph on it in a childlike reflex to persuade myself that it won't be too hot, and drink rapidly, glancing at my watch a couple of times.

Calum looks up slightly and I have no idea what he's thinking for about five calm seconds, until his eyes grow horrifyingly in size behind his magnifying spectacles and he goes a scarlet colour. His mouth opens with a sort of "buh" sound, and blobs of banana and custard dribble down his chin. He thrashes his hands about, looking for a paper napkin. I hold one in front of him but his eyes are streaming and pointing in all sorts of directions, so it is a while before he notices it and grips the serviette, his hand-eye coordination shot out the water by this unhappy experience. I believe I know what the difficulty is, and my suspicions are confirmed when I hear Calum say "Ot! Ot!"

After regaining his composure, he drinks some water and, still chewing, mutters, "Uperheapeb bip becov of ba micwowave." By this time, I am sweating in my seat and biting my lip – although what I feel like doing is rocking back and forth and wailing with laughter like some sort of klaxon. Trying to retrieve his spoon, Clewstrie now discovers that it is stuck fast to the syrup, which in turn is stuck fast to the bowl. To make his point, he lifts the spoon and the entire bowl duly raises itself off the table. "Look at that, Steve, look at it!"

I look at it with suddenly mounting concern and say, "That custard's about to spill…"

As he changes his grip on the spoon, whatever physical or chemical link has formed between the metal cutlery and the non-metal syrup gives up. The bowl falls a few inches to the table, spattering me and Calum with hot custard. A particularly large dollop is catapulted onto the lap of the hapless Clewstrie and, with the instinctive desire to brush the stuff away, he succeeds in scalding himself for the second time in the period of his hot sweet. "Baaaahhhhayyyyyaaaaaaaaaaaaahhhhhhh… FUCK!" he says.

"Undersea Eruption" is the sort of contrived, fatuous, hoping-for-a-disaster porn that makes me want to kick a few Hollywood producers' arses for not having thought up similar gobshite to stick into the cinema so that these poor professional cretins didn't have to be taken down to the mid-Atlantic ridge on some ooh-let's-be-proper-geologists-and-look-at-the-pretty-underwater-rocks pretence and half boiled to death for the entertainment of the bubble-sniggering camera crew and, par extension, *the fat-bottomed viewer. Save proper scientists I say, and don't gratify the ratings by watching this basaltic pus-boil blistering out of your small screen.*

Some day, I suspect, I will give up one job. But it will be the change in ratings that decide, not me.

aphorisms and musings rejected on the grounds of being false,
meaningless, truisms or flawed in some other way

1.   A prediction, or a vain hope?
In 2044, a firm called Sharpy's will transform restaurant culture with
their chain of *restos-vinaigre* and their famous slogan:
"A bucket of balsamic in every recipe!"

2.   Amid chaotic scenes, the Central African Republic beat
Ecuador in the grand final of the Aptly Named Country Awards 1987, and
the Great Powers shrank into renewed impotence.

3.   Crumbledown II, at $225 million, overtakes "Who's Got
Patty's Strudel Now?" as being the most expensive pudding sequel ever
made.

4.   Extreme heat and extreme cold seem identical to you if you
are a mere layman.

5.   Fiction may be termed *literary fiction* if it contains at least
one reference to "brackish water".

6.   How many men must a road be walked on by?
The answer is farting in the bed.

7.   If semiotic intention could be weighed, it would be found to
be denser among the French.

8.   Insert the courgette NOW.

9.   My toenails grow faster than your toenails.

10.   No, that wasn't the most appealing noise ever to have come out of my bottom – but then, none of them are, really.

11.   Not for the first time, I am amazed how much I can enjoy eating lamb.
Sorry. That's probably not very interesting for you.

12.   Robert said, "It's a bit like a hard, crispy sponge." And then he wished he hadn't.

13.   Sneeze onto dry, not wet.

14.   Sperm help make babies.

15.   That really was a pretty nice cup of tea there.

16.   The enjoyment of seasoning on your food is largely psychosomatic. It is an entirely different matter, however, with condiments.
Mmm. Condiments!

17.   The expression "singing from the same hymn sheet" derives from the preposterous behaviour of some old Hanseatic League city councils, which used to hold a rather peculiar form of internal ballot to settle the important issues of the day.
When debating was over and the time had come for voting, each councillor would collect his ballot paper from the proctor and take it into the polling booth, where he would use a pencil to mark a cross against one of the two, or occasionally three, options available. Having thus indicated his vote, the councillor would validate his ballot paper by dipping his thumb in a butter dish of ink (which would be mauve, indigo or crimson, depending on the administrative status of the vote) and "thumbing the corner".
In a panel on one side of the booth were numbered slots, where sets of hymn sheets were provided, corresponding to the two or three voting options. The councillor would withdraw a hymn sheet from the appropriate slot, and would leave the booth, taking care not to let any of his colleagues see the text or music.
The councillors then showed their "crossed and thumbed" voting papers to the proctor before placing them in the ballot box, and would start

to circulate around the polling room, keeping their newly acquired hymn sheets close to their persons. If there were a few minutes to spare and if they could find a quiet corner, they would try to familiarise themselves with the hymn in question if they did not know it already. If they did know it, they were free to converse for a little time with their colleagues, although it was of course forbidden to discuss one's vote (or allocated hymn) explicitly.

After a little time, a *Pauke* would be struck by a brightly uniformed servitor, prompting each councillor to fold his hymn sheet and place it in the "hymns" box, before approaching the deputy proctor to collect their blindfolds.

Upon satisfying himself that all councillors had surrendered their hymn sheets and donned their blindfolds, the servitor would then strike the *Pauke* a second time, prompting the assembly to start rendering their respective hymns unaccompanied.

Councillors hence commenced singing as they stumbled around the room, the aim being to locate and then congregate with others performing the same hymn without knocking their heads together too severely. Burst lips were an occasional occurrence in Visby, it is said; in Bremen, bloody noses were said to be "too frequent a disruption"; in Deventer, councillors traditionally cupped their hands around their ears to aid hymn recognition, which made accidental head butting less frequent, if only at the cost of elbowings in the teeth becoming "a regrettable hazard".

Usually after about a minute, two (or three) well-defined clumps of people would have formed, and would be belting out their respective melodies from their settled areas of the polling room. After what sometimes turned out to be a surprisingly well coordinated crescendo – despite the multiplicity of hymns being sung – blindfolds would be torn off and heated argument, shouting and even fisticuffs would often follow.

18.   The open admiration of pets in public places is responsible for 2.79 per cent of relationships lasting a year or more.

19.   What the hell are the moral chip shops of temptation if they're not actual chip shops?

20.   Yesterday. Another entire day without a second's thought about my lymphatic system.

HOW IT HAPPENED

No partner – pornography.
No pornography – hunger.
No meals – choccy bics.
No choccy bics – milk.
No milk – cheese.
No cheese – crackers.
No crackers – bed.
No sleep – insomnia.

It was this chain of frustration that drove Roderick Potts out onto the street that Tuesday night. It was late October, when everybody in Scotland below the age of 50 is still childishly surprised about how early it is getting dark, in exactly the same way that they are taken aback to see a flurry of December snow. Hence, imagining it to be almost midnight, Roddy was surprised and delighted to see that his phone was showing 21.55, which meant he could perhaps pop into Mo Iqbal's. He could get a men's magazine – the expensive promise of tanned and oiled eye gum for the irredeemably straight noughties Brit-lad – a four-pack of Heineken, a lottery scratchcard and some sort of microwaveable snack. On the other hand, he could convince himself that he need not follow such a stereotypical bachelor lifestyle and, through self-control, opt for only two out of the above.

"How you doing?" he addressed Mo, confidently reaching for *FHM*. Mentally, he was patting himself on the back for not going for something off the top shelf. He had restrained his other purchases to two cans of Budweiser and a single lottery scratchcard.

Out of the shop and onto Great Western Road's expansive pavement, he took the scratchie out of his wallet and started at it with a 2p coin. Despite the relative quiet of that particular stretch of the grand and famous boulevard, he was jarred with self-consciousness, since he had never before seen any other human being play a lottery scratchcard in a public place – although he was convinced it must happen sometimes.

He rubbed the grey guck off the six numbers in the predictable fashion: left to right on the top row, then the middle row, then the bottom row. He had a theory about never winning on one of these things by revealing the bottom right number last but, that night, his theory was disproved: in that very corner, the third "£17.00 SVNTN" revealed itself.

On his childhood trips to Rothesay, Largs and Elie, Roddy had noticed that a little wave breaking on the sand can often be overwhelmed by a bigger one that overtakes it at the last moment. And such was his emotional experience on looking up from the little field of vision containing the modestly victorious scratchcard, the coin and his two hands to see, no more than one second later, his ex-girlfriend, Gail McHarg, turn her head towards him. Because she was behind the toughened glass of a bus shelter, it was almost like she was only on television. After she came round the corner of the shelter, however, she became corporeal.

She looked beautiful. The blonde hair was a bit shorter and straighter; pure, intelligent blue eyes; two perfect petals of lipstick. Replacing her phone in her neat little (new) handbag, she looked at him with an expression just short of a smile. Too bad there was no discernible warmth or comfort in the respective glances.

A frown of disapproval quickly took over Gail's face. "I see you haven't changed," she said, nodding towards the top corner of Roddy's *FHM*, which was protruding out of his cornershop-blue plastic bag. The comment baffled him, as he was sure he had never had such a publication on display in his flat on any occasion when Gail had been there.

"But I guess I never really knew you."

Ouch.

What?

No – he was right the first time: Ouch.

"How are you?" she then asked. An almost caring non sequitur to her previous volley of words.

"Dunno, really," was what came out of his mouth. He realised immediately that was a useless, rather hostile, and possibly even weird, answer. "Well, fine," he revised.

She looked at him blankly. He had become the half-way point to some middle distance for her. "How have you been?" he found himself saying.

"Fine," she replied, with something of a harsh tone. "You should come round to my flat," she added. It was a cold, almost robotic, command, and quite unexpected. In fact, she might as well have been some sort of decoy cyborg Gail, instructed simply to remind him she wasn't his any more.

The middle three weeks of their relationship had been pretty marvellous. Before and after had been halting, nervy and uncommunicative from both sides. Par for the course for Roddy.

"Hang on a minute," she indicated, letting some humanity peep out of her, breaking her enigmatic spell. "If I'm not going to get this bus I'll need to tell the person at the other end."

"Other end?" What? But Roddy did not ask what she meant by that – it would have been the wrong thing to do. She hid herself round the far end of the bus shelter and talked on her mobile for fully seven minutes, giggling every so often, which made Roddy feel nervous to the extent of his throat going dry and his feeling slightly faint. And a bit bored, too.

"Let's go," she said after she'd finished. To his confusion and pleasure, she slipped her arm around his, and his grip on reality got a wee bit floaty. He was barely sure of the direction they were setting off in. His brain was trying, of course, to sidestep the obvious issues, like whether they still had feelings for each other, what she had really said to his mate Tony during that mad night at the boozer after they'd all went to see "The Fellowship of the Ring" and whether that clown Baz could get it up, what with all the rumours. Instead, he became fixated on whether they were going to walk all the way to where they were going and on the change he would need for any bus they might be going on.

They walked for something like half an hour. The streets were mostly lined with reddish tenements, as streets in this city often are. They passed two sets of shops, but Roddy's head was so taken up with the task of producing smalltalk that he ignored his urges to go into somewhere and buy some Coke or Irn-Bru or something. Chips would have been nice, he mused, not least when they passed I Know You Got Sole, which was doing a brisk trade.

"Your sister got into Strathclyde all right, then?"

"Yeah, yeah. She's really pleased with the course so far. Still a bit shy, but."

"Yeah."

"Right, up you come."

She inserted her key into what might as well have been a random front door.

Her new flat. Who'd be there, then? The boyfriend? Flatmates?

It was one of those stairs whose tiles just had to be creamy yellow and brown. She led him to the first-floor landing. As the door opened, he glimpsed a dark-haired girl going past. She wore a blue hair band and a dull-coloured skirt. She glanced into his eyes, and glanced out of them again, depositing no particular expression. The cistern in the toilet could be heard re-filling.

Roddy sat down at the kitchen table, as he was prompted to do. He put the plastic bag on the floor in front of his feet, trying to hide the now thoroughly embarrassing magazine by getting it to slip down as far as it would go. If he was going to assert himself as a decisive, independent individual, he should surprise her by updating her on - say - a change of drinking habit. Unfortunately, however, such a thing had not happened. And there, after all, was that beer in his bag. As it was, he simply waited to accept the milky tea she made for him so perfectly.

"You seen anyone since me, then?"

What a dreadful question. He didn't reckon the answer could be relevant, no matter what it actually was, and he didn't like being asked.

He shook his head. "You know me," he said. She frowned. "I won't tell you about my couple of near misses in Clarty Pat's," he added, using his favoured, somewhat genteel, pronunciation for the famous nightspot.

"No," she said. "I don't need to know, right enough."

Another flatmate appeared at the door and put her head and an arm into the kitchen, clearly enquiring whether she was interrupting a private conversation and whether it would be okay if she got herself some tea. It wasn't the one Roddy had glimpsed a couple of minutes before. Gail smiled at her and gave her some sort of nod and, indeed, wink. "Come and join us."

Roddy looked over at her and smiled politely, expecting to be introduced to this rather handsome, blondish young woman. She got out what he guessed to be her favourite mug, which featured a scuffed picture of Fran Healy. She looked at him for a couple of seconds and said, "Well, Roddy, I've been reliably informed that I'm your type."

If he had been looking at a picture of her or had passed her in the street, he would definitely have noted her as being quite attractive, but his current feeling, under these circumstances, was one of queasy terror and not a little astonishment.

Gail made him turn first crimson, and then white: "Do you think you're old enough to hold onto a good thing?"

"I…" It took a few seconds to work out the correct principle behind the answer to this.

"Yes." Not especially eloquent. He lowered his eyes.

"Good. I'll see you round, then," went Gail, and walked out of the kitchen, leaving Roddy open mouthed, like a fish with an open mouth. She could be heard leaving the flat and letting the heavy front door down below swing shut a quarter of a minute later.

"Listen," Jennifer said, "I've heard Gail's side of it, and I don't honestly think anyone would expect you to have done anything different in the circumstances." Roddy's mouth was still open, as if that offered him some sort of biological coping mechanism for finding himself in surreal conversations like this one. "She'll always be a lovely bit of your history now."

"Yes," said Roddy, warmed by this approach, but wishing he had a few more words in him than that.

"I think we should go out for a drink."

"Okay, then. Em. Sure. Em..."

"My name? My name's Jennifer. I'm really pleased to meet you at last."

And that's how it happened.

THE EASTERN TALE OF DEATH

The guy just sort of sidled up to me in the Cat's Cradle, which is the second closest bar to my house. The Flower Basket, which is next-door to my stair and boasts the finest pub lunch in the east of the Shire, is far too family-oriented for midday alcoholics such as myself.

Anyway. The guy, a balding man of medium size and shape – much like myself – spoke plainly and eagerly: "Went through to the east coast day before yesterday there. Got the Edinburgh train and then on to Dunbar, on the London train. Guess what?"

I was already experiencing some difficulty tuning in to this suddenly commenced narration, and was struggling also with the usual uncertainty: whether or not to open myself to the familiarity with which I was approached. Coping with the drastic "guess what" at the end, with its heavy-duty punctuation, especially after that barrage of travel information, was quite beyond my verbal powers, so I just nodded, flicking my eyebrows a few millimetres up the way so as to invite the guy to continue.

"Saw a funeral happening. Do you know where Musselburgh is?"

Again, I was dumbfounded, this time by the uncomfortable if not baffling juxtaposition of the macabre statement and the geographical query. However, I was now able to muster a reply: "Musselburgh's near Edinburgh."

"Just to the east of Edinburgh," he said, in a tone that informed me that my answer was at best inadequate if not plain wrong. "We were whizzing past Musselburgh, the train getting faster and faster, and in the space of one or two seconds I saw a gathering of black-dressed people standing around a rectangular trough. You could just make out the minister on the inside of the gathering. You know? Nobody was moving. They were listening to the minister. Or priest, I suppose – I'm not sure.

"You know," he continued, dealing me another disconcerting surprise, "my family is pregnant with death."

I must have been properly drawn into his conversation by that stage, because I found myself saying, "How d'you m—", but he was obviously going to answer anyway.

"Many of my relatives are very, very old."

"Really?" I found myself asking, still wary that our dialogue had no legitimate – to my standards – foundation, such as an introduction, previous acquaintance or some commonly held focus, such as a cortège going along the street outside, which might have been an appropriate prompt for his particular line of chat.

"My Auntie Matilda" he went on – I had always thought 'aunt' should go with trisyllabic names like Matilda, but never mind – "is one hundred and three." This reduced me to nodding again. "My grandmother is one hundred and five – she lives out by Nitshill now," – *by* Nitshill?!? – "and old Ethel, a cousin of my 108-year-old grandfather, is one hundred and ten."

"Well, I must say," I remarked, "It does sound as though the genes in your family are pretty well disposed towards longevity," – I immediately grew concerned that I was stating the obvious – "and you have every right to expect a good stretch ahead of you. In fact, I'd be surprised if those ages aren't a record for one family. At least a national or... or a Scottish record, anyway," I continued, descending quickly into self-consciousness about my own rather wittery part in this dialogue.

"Your academic background has led you to be over-analytical, my friend," he announced, astonishing me to the greatest degree in the conversation so far.

"And *your* academic background has led you the same way, I would guess," I riposted, piqued that the guy had been sizing up my accent. This time, I was quite taken aback by my own answer. The guy then grabbed my arm. Drastically changing the orientation of the lines on his face, he proceeded to chuckle solidly for some five to six seconds.

"I haven't told you the worst of it, though," he said once he had finished, releasing his grip on my arm as his facial features re-tuned to a less jocular arrangement. "My other grandmother, on my father's side, Tabatha McNeill, is one hundred and fourteen next week."

At this point, I felt unable to listen further. It was as if a switch had been flicked. My incredulity had surpassed its limit. In short: from that instant, I no longer believed a single word he was saying to me.

"Tell me, what do—"

"Name's Danny."

"Tell me, Danny, what do you do for a living?"

149

"Why?" he asked, as if he was never asked this sort of question.

Just asking, I thought; "No, it's alright, it doesn't matter," I said.

Although I risk soon running out of expressions to convey my ongoing and escalating surprise, the guy's next comment just about bowled me over. It was this:

"I interviewed you for a job once."

I became cross at this point, and was close to telling him directly that I didn't believe a single thing he had said, but instead I called his bluff.

"What for? What year?"

"Five year ago." He leant back towards me, with a smug, creased-up face of satisfaction, and added, "for the job at the building society."

I raised my voice now. "Hah! I worked at the Bank of Scotland for two years when I was in my twenties, a long time ago. Not a building society. I have never done anything else in the financial or property sectors – I sell top-of-the-range sports equipment now, thank you very much. I'm sorry, mate, but I think you're a fraud."

A change swept over the guy's whole ill-shaven expression, like a field of stubble that had been baked for hours by warm sunshine getting slaked by a cold, sleet-drenched cloud. "And," I added, "I bet you send yourself birthday cards from all these phoney aunties and grannies you don't really have. You…" – the insult came slowly and a little disjointedly – "you quack!"

That broke him. I polished off my Carlsberg, stood up and left him sobbing at the bar.

South Shores

Bay on the far shore
Crescents the sun and
Beaches the fishing boats.
It gives sand to the wind.

Forest beyond the mountains
Hosts the birds and
Hides the fugitives.
It rakes the wind.

Lake in the next country
Bears up the kayaks and
Nourishes the rivers.
It ripples with the wind.

This building
Houses me and
Holds me inside.
It shuts the wind out.

dream sequence idea #1

Close-up of gameshow host spinning a big wheel. He appears to be Armando Iannucci.

IANNUCI: Round and round the Cheese Wheel goes! Where will it stop…?

AUDIENCE: Nobody knows!

Terrified contestant watches self-pityingly as his preferred options of Leerdammer and Gruyère slip tantalisingly past in their little triangular compartments.

IANNUCI: Ha ha!

The arrow comes to rest next to a pale yellow block of Spanish cheese labelled "Fuerte," which Iannucci grabs off the edge of the wheel and proceeds to stuff into the contestant's mouth. The contestant writhes around on the studio floor in great distress while the gameshow host, who has now become a larger, red-faced, bearded man, sniggers and cackles.

THE GRINBERG AVENUE CASE

I'm fuckin half way through lighting up my cigarette when the telephone rings. It's like a reminder I'm trying to quit, so I stub the fucker out in the ashtray after taking my one and only drag.

"This is Jim Bookbinder," I croak into the receiver.

"Bookbinder. We need you right away. It's a murder."

I register the information without emotional reaction. It's a job.

"Where?"

"Three seventeen Grinberg Avenue."

"You're fuckin kiddin me."

"I know, I know. Just get over here first – we'll give you some time at the scene later."

"I'll be right there."

Jesus, the inspector sounds tense. I get in my car and start wondering what or who could have disturbed sleepy Grinberg Avenue – also known locally as Geriatric Boulevard – with a homicide. And on a Tuesday, too. I'm thinking a panicking burglar is the most likely culprit.

The guys in the station can't help staring at the goddam cigarette hanging out of my mouth when I stroll into the office. All the desk boys look up – it's still not long since the Vinko Slapnik case, which ended in the big bad Slovene finally getting time for his ten armed robberies – and my Uncle Larry being run over by the groceries truck I had requisitioned.

That had been a confusing case all right, with what I can only describe as a mixed outcome, and everyone here at 1313 Carter Street – known locally as the Unlucky House – was trying so damn hard to be understanding that I sometimes felt like walking out, or yelling or doing some damn thing.

The inspector is pacing his twelve feet of office. "Where's

Bookbinder? He was meant to be here ten minutes ago." He has his back turned to me as I open the door.

"Bookbinder's right here, *sir*," I report, throwing my coat onto the seat.

"God dammit, Bookbinder," he raises his voice, "where's that hit-and-run report you were supposed to file by yesterday?"

"Where it's safest," I reply, tapping the side of my head.

"Does the word deadline mean anything to you, Bookbinder?"

"Deadline? I ain't dead yet. Now, do you want that report or not? And what about this murder?"

"All right, Bookbinder, just take a seat." As if I ever do. "We've got a homicide at 317 Grinberg. Now get this: ornaments, several hundred dollars in cash in the dresser, under a mattress and in other obvious locations, jewelry likewise, some small, easy-to-carry items of artwork and more than just a trace of cocaine sitting on a table..."

"You're about to tell me none of it was touched, Chief."

I take out my lighter and burn a few shreds of Virginia tobacco leaf while the inspector wipes his face with the back of his hand, frowning as he fails to hide his irritation.

"OK. Now the old lady was seventy years old. But it's the method that I ain't never seen before."

"You intrigue me, Chief."

"Quit the backchat, Bookbinder, for Christ's sake... Have you ever heard of death by screwdriver?"

"Sure, last year a..."

"No, I mean screwing a sharpened screw into the throat and slowly taking it out again, letting the victim – who we figure would already be kinda distressed – bleed to death from a pierced jugular."

I take a big draw, gaze deep into the smoldering end of my cigarette, and look around for an ashtray. Dalford, who is temporarily replacing Stuart Grady, my usual partner, who got stepped on by an elephant during our investigation into the heroin-smuggling zookeepers case, picks up my eyes and gets one from the desk of the secretaries' room next-door.

"Methodical. A little messy. Unusual," I concede.

"Goddam right, Bookbinder. Now get yourself to the location and then go see some witnesses."

"Mrs Elder?"

The old dear in the apartment downstairs from the scene takes one look at me before she starts closing the door again and shaking her head at the same time. I'm pretty surprised, but I guess it's just another office fuck-up. I turn round and –

"It's Miss Elder, I'll think you'll find." She tuts, visibly projecting saliva in front of her.

You have to think fast in situations like these.

"Will you accept an apology, Miss Elder? Our people back at headquarters can be dreadfully remiss. I do wonder at their lack of attention to detail sometimes."

The door opens up again and the old dame's eyebrows rustle upwards a little. Soon I'm inside, with a cup of tea in my hand. The tea is barely warm and I'll swear the milk is sour, but I take the beverage as an important sign of trust.

"It happened about 2 am, didn't it, Miss Elder?"

She blinks and reflects carefully about the thought she's forming.

"You're here about that murder last night."

"Yes, Miss Elder, yes I am."

Miss Elder was a lively old bird, with the quickest wisecracks this side of the metropolitan area. It wasn't until the next day that I found out a couple more things about her and came up with the idea of getting out of the police department to work in stationery like I do now.

I got her statement, which was nothing much more than times, vague noises, and so on. The usual tentative looking out through the drapes and supposedly seeing jack shit.

Anyhow, the tea was followed by another, and I was given one of those terrible offers of cake which you just can't refuse in the police business – training doesn't cover that sort of situation. It was full of dried fruit and, I figured, walnut.

I left with a mild headache and started wondering if I'd had enough sleep. Suffice to say the headache was just the start, and I found myself going home, not back to the Unlucky House.

"Bookbinder? Are you awake now?"

I was still pretty nauseous, and even speaking into the telephone made me feel terrible.

"If you're sick, you're sick, Bookbinder, but phone the next time, huh?… What's that? Right. And which witness did you see?… Downstairs neighbor, you say? Right. Huh? What was the first name? Just a minute – I'll call you back."

The Chief was back on the phone in five minutes, unfortunately when I was trying to take a dump, but we got back in contact soon enough.

I'd never been good with names. One time, on an undercover mission, I had called Ronald "Bigface" MacRae "Bigmouth" by mistake, and that was just what I ended up with. I could only eat half-heated-up pepperoni pizza for a week, and gastro-enteritis followed. What a goof-up.

" . . . And do you know what?" Chief sounded angry again.

"You intrigue…"

"Shuddup. Did you know that this Sylvia Elder is wanted for food poisoning in three states? Doesn't that name ring a bell? Don't you watch the news? In fact, do you ever look at the main noticeboard in the office? The one with that big picture of the old lady?"

"C'mon, Chief, it wasn't the most obvious question at the time, you know – 'Can I just check: are you a communist or a serial poisoner, ma'am?' – although lately, I find myself wondering if some people–"

"BOOKBINDERRRRRR……!!!!"

"Chief, I wish you wouldn't yell at me like that. I get real nervous when I'm sick."

"All right, Bookbinder, take it easy. Will you be in a fit state to go to the old dame's house again tomorrow? Ashford's there right now, but Elder's gone."

"I don't know, Chief. My ass is like a hot tap at the…"

"For the love of Christ, Bookbinder, spare me the details, huh? Jeez!"

"I don't know about tomorrow, but…"

"I tell you what, Bookbinder, just forget this one, huh?"

"I'm off the case?"

"You sure are."

"Am I off the Delaney case too, Chief?"

"Why not?" he barked, and slammed the phone down. Sheesh! What a mood.

And with a combination of attitude and recurring gastric illness, I persuaded the police department to let me go a couple of months later. I now deal with wholesale office supplies, partly because of the insecurity I was suffering on account of no longer smoking. Little did I dream, however, that a few years down the line the world of ball-point pen retail would bring me back face to face with Sylvia Elder, and little did anyone know then about her involvement in the fascinating underworld of poison ink, in which she was one of the true, inspired leaders.

But I guess that's a story for another time.

THE TREATY

"And I am Mr Moronty," beamed Mr Moronty. As he shook my hand, his head and his right shoulder tilted down towards the cheap-looking chairs that cluttered the central part of the room.

His grip turned out to be firm. This came as little surprise: his wide face and his big long arms did not look like those of a weak man. He added, "We met briefly last year, in fact," which was quite true, I now realised.

A much thinner man, called Balby, gave me a brisker handshake, saying, "Glad you could make it," with an impish flexing of the eyebrows that told me he rarely said much funnier things than this. He was of course alluding to the absence of Irena Karstalon (serious injury of son in coach crash) and also of her deputy, Markus Tersalaron (failure of the plane to get off the runway on Slatell Island), and to my consequent and unexpected presence there.

"May we talk to you about the outstanding points?" beamed Moronty, his walnut head still cocked slightly to one side.

"Well," I replied, quite nervous, but trying to get into the swing of things, "let me present things to you as we see them."

Surprisingly, at least to me, Moronty's head then tilted all the way over to the opposite side, perhaps signalling its switching over into receive mode. The smile was wide and solid, held in place by firm facial muscles that I suspected had chewed regularly and often on fruit, fresh vegetables and, I dare say, nuts. He didn't need to add "Go ahead," but did so in a warm basso.

"Mr Farshakhon believes that we should be able to maintain our citizenship – our individual authority, if you will. If we do not know... that is... if we can't know ourselves, we can't respect ourselves, and we have no way... that is, no means of – "

At this point, I was interrupted by Mr Balby, which was fortunate, for I might not have finished my sentence anyway. Sweat was forming upon my forehead and my eyes were swimming around somewhat, failing to provide me with a coherent view of the room. "Well, look," Balby said. "You join us under one constitution and president; we will safeguard your identity." I had wanted a conjunction in the middle there, but he gave none. "You keep all your international sports teams, your TV channels," he proffered, adding, "It's important, these things," at half the volume and with grammar that annoyed me further.

"And here's something you'll like." Elevating himself with this forthcoming offer, Balby at once seemed a bigger man in my field of vision. "You guys have our passports, but with your own unique designation of citizenship stated right underneath the coat of arms on the front – right there," he said, pointing to his own document to demonstrate. "This secures the individual to certain rights. Access to your schools. All the culture stuff I talked to Mr Farshakhon about previously. If your people have the impression that they're not getting ruled from some far-off capital out west, then that becomes the reality. That, in turn, reinforces the impression. And so on."

"But," I started, with no idea as to what words were to follow. Balby seemed at this point to perceive what a nuisance all the chairs were, blocking off the centre of the room between the two big desks and making it a useless space. People wouldn't sit so close together like that anyway.

As for Moronty, he was no longer smiling. He had started peering at his left hand as if there were something wrong with it, or as if he couldn't quite get over how big it was, flipping it over and back again like some great bat he had just discovered was appended to the end of his arm. My daughter, meanwhile, was still standing looking out of one of the bigger windows, up at the top end of the room.

I had lost the thread of the conversation, such as it was, and felt no control over any questions or answers that might be about to come out of my mouth.

"Our assembly," I found myself saying.

"Without secession powers of course," clipped Balby, avoiding my gaze, his legs uncrossing and his eyes darting to the upper, grimier parts of the nearest art deco window frame. By now he was perched up on the edge of one of the big desks, his errant feet trying to make use of a couple of the nearby chairs.

Frankly, the thing was a fait accompli, and we were in essence going over well-trodden ground, but the press needed some venue and time to identify as "final negotiations".

I lowered my head, the handover of a quarrelsome chunk of snowy-wet land making me feel giddy and childish. I couldn't help thinking of the matter-of-fact narration of all this in history tomes in years to come. I supposed I would get top billing on one of those hour-long television documentaries where people speak about their crucial roles in recent history before they pop off, holding forth in some well-furnished lounge or opulent study, in front of a bookcase. "The autonomous province should do as it likes and say as it likes," I asserted. "We should be able to have pink post boxes with lime-green spots if we want to," I clarified.

"That's quite up to you entirely," intoned Moronty, the warmth deep in him, but without any hint of having been in the slightest bit tickled by this particular suggestion.

I was hit at this point by a further pang of insecurity, as I thought how important the moment was for me not even to have brought a pen. Our officials and private secretaries were excluded from this wing of the building – they might as well have been taking an hour off. Perhaps they were, for all I knew. I looked up to the far end of the room. "Are you coming home tonight?" I called out to my daughter, who was still looking out the window.

"Um," she said, taking a few seconds to finish staring at some tree or other object in the broad swathe of curtilage. "I'll probably see you again in about two weeks' time." Her tone put it somewhere between a statement and a question.

"Sure. That's, um... " A second or two later I silently mouthed the word "fine" to finish the sentence for my own syntactic comfort. The one time I had actually seen Moronty's great hand swallowing up hers, life had stood still for me. Now, my memory replayed that vision.

"Perhaps a walk in the gardens," I suggested, catching Moronty's eye. "I must say I could do with a spot of fresh air," I explained, although I could feel the approach of a stronger urge – to be alone.

Moronty, and to a lesser extent Balby, exuded ever greater levels of warmth. Janie seemed to want to stay in the room. She had sat up on one of the big desks now and was dangling her legs off it, rather like Balby had been doing moments before.

A helicopter was evident once we were outside, buzzing right above our heads, and I imagined the correspondents explaining that everything was all confirmed and that it would all be changing in a calm sort of way by Christmas-time next year, as had already been substantially agreed.

I sat down on one of the benches set among the rhododendrons, Moronty on one side of me and Balby on the other. "I think we're there," I thought of saying to them. I also thought it would be appropriate to slap them both on the shoulders in affirmation. But I was too weary. I could feel energy draining out of me into them, or out into the gardens somewhere. I think I said "It's all fine" or something, but I can't even remember. We all knew everything was done and dusted.

Not long afterwards I got through the clot of microphones and flashbulbs at the gates, climbed into the waiting car and got driven down the lane and along the short stretch of motorway. I muttered grateful and exhausted greetings to my hosts, made my excuses, changed into my pyjamas and clambered up into the soft, raised bed in the corner of the room. I slept for some thirteen hours.

POLLOKSHAWS ROAD

He scrutinised every part of his face using the touch of his right hand. Still quite a fresh shave.

It had been this morning's fingers that had held the razor. That was an altogether more innocent time, breakfast time this morning.

He put his jacket back on, having carried it here over his right shoulder. Quite clean, his jacket. But the person who had brushed it with that lump of metal bristles stuck onto a plastic handle had done so with this morning's briskness.

He looked down, staring at the kerb, not distracted by any high heel or bus wheel or dropped 20p piece. He needed just a few extra seconds. He let the man with the suit and the beer-tugged tie go on first. Only then could he contemplate raising his eyes to communicate his part of the contract: that of a passenger going back to an empty house. Empty, save that it surely still contained some faded warmth from her breath.

"One ninety, pal," he'd manage. Then he'd sit motionlessly, sharing a seat with someone else if absolutely necessary, waiting patiently to start unravelling on the second-last 38 bus of the day.

WRITING TO IVANKO

Bobby sat down. "Right," he said to himself, as he always did at the beginning of a new task.

And the task of the moment was to locate a town in Bulgaria, near somewhere called Burgas.

It was a pretty crap crossword. It wasn't really a question of general knowledge; it was all to do with the quality of your atlases and encyclopaedias or whether or not you had a computer and a modem at home, which Bobby didn't think was very fair. Still, Carlo at the work had made it up himself – he'd been spotted in the library in the town, which had raised a few eyebrows – and it was all for the showroom benevolent fund. Do the crossword, hand it in with your fiver and the winner takes half.

Bobby put "towns near Burgas" into the Google. He already had two of the letters, so it was obvious that he had got the right place from a quick glance at the first page of results. He mentally patted himself on the back for his instinct and his recent loss of fear about using the PC. It was an interesting variety of pages that had come up, including some really slick sites for local municipalities, with fancy tabs and metallic-coloured drop-down menus that went swoosh when you clicked on them. There was also one or two with the likes of "Would you like to meet young beautiful Bulgarian girls?" He thought about it for a few seconds before going onto the second page of results.

There was his wee town come up again on someone's page. Click.

"Dearie dear," he said out loud. There was a small photo of an unremarkable-looking young man with brown eyes, thick eyebrows and sort of 80s-looking short dark hair. It was a poor site, with a few buttons down the left-hand side with some writing in that funny-looking Bulgarian or Russian alphabet or whatever it was, and then a description of the wee teenage nyaff under the picture to the right, attempted in English.

Hi, everybody!

My name is Ivanko Markov. I live in village Troyanovo. My birth date 13 April 1981. I now leave High School and I want very much go to studying in Plovdiv in this University. My father is factory manager in Burgas City. Girls! Now I have fast Opel car belonging to family. I can take you riding in it many times, if you like. Write!

I like also the horse riding and motorbikes and I go one time to F1 with my friend Hristo. Nurburgring kiks ass!!!!!

You want to write in guest book? Please! Write! I write you back very soon. I like Chemistry and lots Wood Works inside school. What you do like?

One day I just want to go to US. Just biking across the country!!!!

Stay cool!

Ivanko

The next morning, Bobby walked across the showroom floor with a twinkle in his eye. He started to whistle as he went through the door into the back office, and he continued to do so as he sat down. He hung his jacket up on the peg and pushed the button to start his now prehistoric device. Windows 95 grunted and clicked into life while he got his first Klix coffee from the other machine. Such was the morning ritual.

After a few minutes it was ready for him to open up the e-mail and put his humanitarian idea into action.

"Guys,

Check out this guy's site. Think he could do with some correspondence!"

He copied and pasted in the link and sent it round his colleagues, opened up the draft sales report he'd started work on yesterday, which he was going to have to get a move on with, and went through to Sandy's end of the office to ask him about his son's graduation, still thinking about the difference that could be made to a young person's life by a bit of communication and interest.

"Hey, Boaby, awright?"

"Aye. How wis the graduation thair?"

"Grand. Great day oot. Chatted tae a few other parents, eh. Lots ay overseas, ken, an Irish an that. Eh... What's this? Where'd ye get that website fae? Is that fir real?"

"Mind ay that crossword that Stan's sent roon that Carlo did fir the benevolent night?"

"Aye. Ah've no done it yet, but. Huv you?"

"Aye, that's me away tae haun it in. Wan ay thae questions is aboot Bulgaria, ken, an Ah fun yon site when Ah wis lookin oan the internet fir thon toon thair."

"It's a laugh, eh."

"Aye."

And then Bobby went to Stan and handed over the fiver and the crossword.

"What's this? Something to do with that Bulgaria question, is it?" asked Stan, looking up from his screen. Jack Ruthven and Tommy Barnes had been heard roaring with laughter from their desks.

"Aye. It's a laugh, eh?" suggested Bobby.

"Hmm," thought and said Stan.

That sales report took him forever, and he had no choice but to really get into it. Then Malcolm from the Leith store gave him this shitty sourcing job to do, which required loads of e-mails and calls. It was Thursday before he went back and saw how young Ivanko's site was doing.

Dougald, Bridge of Allan, Scotland, UK: Hi there, Ivanko. Do you like Jazz? I'm a really big Blue Note fan myself. It's Freddie Hubbard I probably admire the most. Do you know him? There's a man you've got to admire for perseverance. He's still got plenty of energy left in him! Anyway, you must put something on your site about what music you're into.

Ivanko: Hi Dougald!!! You are my first writer from Scotland. We know your country very much. Do you wear kilt? I see Scottish men on television who have visited Sofia and they have all weared them. Crazy!!!! I like now the acid jazz very much. Do you like?

Mangaboy, Scotland: Oh, kilts, is it? Listen here, chuff arse, I don't own a kilt and none of my pals do. Okay, a couple of them do, but only for going to Wembley and that. And Eck's wedding. But don't get any funny ideas. Got any fanny yet, by the way?

I was meaning to ask there, chuffpants. What's it like to drive a proper car, eh? What is it you are used to there? Do you drive Ladas and shite like that usually? I really hope you get your hole soon, chuffbag, because you are one sad case, by the way. Does your dad let you drink vodka before driving yon big car?

Oh, and remember to use a condom with all those dusky Bulgarian lassies. If you cannae get them in your country, I can send you some whisky-flavoured ones from my country.

And Dougald, if you're watching, turn the fucking dial, eh? See Ivanko? He's got the right idea. Go into your local music shop and ask for the best acid jazz they've got in store, and they'll put you right in no time.

Ivanko: Mangaboy, you Scottish writer also??!! Yes, we have Skoda and Lada, but old. Now we have many cars. You been in Wembley??!! I dream to go. What is fanny? You very much like acid jazz too, I think. Do you listen Massive Attack? New Jersey Kings? I prefer vodka whisky.

Mangaboy, Scotland: What is fanny? Sums you up, Ivan, mate. Gie's your address and I'll send you some of those whisky condoms in the post. Your old man had better have some of them too just to make sure they don't make any more of you. And you shouldn't mix your drinks, as I'm sure your mother tells you. Where do you think Dougald has got to? Maybe he's up in his bedroom playing his trumpet.

Stanley, Scotland: Jack, if this is you, you'll be wanting to drop into my office. And you, Bobby. IMMEDIATELY.

*

Ivanko took another deep breath, looked over towards the lavatory doors and mopped the perspiration off his top lip with his napkin. He had ordered the moussaka and a side dish of asparagus for the main course, although he didn't understand all the French words. Her starter was a sort of fish – what was it called in English? His was *terrine*, in French again.

That had really surprised him about the menu.

She came back from the toilet, putting a mobile telephone back into her handbag.

"Ah," Ivanko commented. "You have cellphone? In my country only businessmans have. Maybe some more people. My friends: only two... hmm... three have."

"Really?" she responded. "Well, I'd say most people in London are using them nowadays."

"I think in two thousands year, everybody will has this."

She blinked for a second, letting Ivanko appreciate her eye shadow and mascara. "By the year 2000? Yes, I expect so." She smiled broadly, revealing her wonderful teeth. "Not so long to wait now, is it?"

Ivanko shifted in his seat, looking down for a moment at his stone-washed jeans, still a bit self-conscious about how much better dressed she was.

"Ivanko," she said, in the sort of clear voice that would sound nice to hear on the radio, perhaps in a drama on the BBC World Service, which he'd spent so much time listening to last week.

"Yes. Julia."

"It's a bit tricky for me to get a train home after 11 o'clock—"

"Oh. I walk with you to station soon. I mean, after we finish in this restaurant."

"No, no," she smiled. He felt her fingertips on his right knee. "I've booked a room in a hotel for the night."

"Hotel?" He could feel his throat going dry instantly.

"I hope you're going to join me, Ivanko."

"Come with you?"

Her smile grew in volume. "I do hope so. And they've got a very nice bar there, for a night cap."

"Night cap," Ivanko repeated. "This is hat?"

"I'd like to have another drink with you, Ivanko, after we've finished our meal."

He nodded. She could see him mouthing the English words, repeating the ones he wasn't sure of, trying desperately to learn for her. "Yes," he said.

"And I know something we could do tomorrow," she added.

"Ah," Ivanko started, sitting up straight with raised eyebrows, having

166

clearly thought of something specific. "Tomorrow in England is... mmm... *golyama nagrada*... In French is *grand prix*."

"The grand prix. That's right."

"What you say in English? The big..."

"Oh, no, we say it in French, too: the grand prix."

"Ah. Okay. Many things you say by French words. I know it will on the television. Man on plane told me this."

She leaned down and pulled the tickets out of her handbag. They said "Silverstone" in big letters right across the top.

First of all, Ivanko just gasped. Then, he started giggling uncontrollably, his face creasing and expanding into a shape that was so unlike the serious, half-melancholic declaration of youth that the whole world knew.

"That's the great thing about the internet, isn't it?" Julia said. "I already know what you like, you see?"

She enjoyed her third mouthful of the Falanghina, and thanked the waiter for her monkfish starter.

"Thank you," Ivanko said, his eyes lowered. He picked up his cutlery, looking at the terrine and lettuce leaves in front of him, worrying that he might not be able stop his fork-holding hand from shaking. "Thank you," he said again.

Leaving St Fillans

Walking west along the contour line,
I take a look upslope.
The foliage being denuded by winter, a sheep track reveals itself,
Leading upwards.
Intrigued by this discovery of another little byway so close to home,
I mount the Girron's incline,
Knowing that I will soon strike the familiar zig-zags.
I keep my head raised,
Anticipating the moment when
My boots add their mark to the surface of the snaking track.

Attentive, I bear witness to its audacious appearance
On the cleared stage of this evening's sky:
The coldest scimitar of projected light,
Bright-sudden enough to be called a flash,
Resting momentarily just yon.
The same flash that has lasted the aeons,
Weightless, pure light girdling the mountain flank.
For a second its nature is mysterious.
My breath leaves me in a gasp.
Then, effortless clarity:

Freakishly distant,
Old familiar globe that has brightened
Billions of eyes and mine.
Ancient grey dust,
By raindrop and zephyr unstirred,
Sings a white soprano chorus
In vacuum silence,
Solar radiance reflected on
The bone-naked airless hairless scalp
Floating easily off Breadalbane's shoulder
As I march higher to assist its elevation.

That lunar face
(he is a distant uncle for us all)
Offers me the dilated eyes of a much
Older man's concern,
Leaving me miniaturised in the
Pitiful youth of decades.

It is time to begin what I have walked out here to do.
So I rehearse words of comfort, hope and love
To convey to those whom I am about to leave,
This duty supervised by
None other than the rising, shining moon.

BRODSKY

or

THE UNORDERED PASTRIES

Brodsky's apartment is contained in a large city. Through this large city flows a sizeable river, into which a smaller one flows, from the north.

It is the biggest city in the country. It is a working city. There are factories; there are offices. There is poverty; there is richness. There is the great in-between. There are good people, and there are good people whose natures have become corrupted.

In the city are situated parks and gardens. Through tunnels clatter trains. Money changes hands on its pavements; little children cry from balconies, ten, twenty storeys up or more. Most places are safe, even at night, but a few corners are better avoided. Alcohol is allowed. It is sold in plenty. Men drink too much of it, and they sometimes carelessly harm other men, and women, and children.

People rise and fall in their workinglife spheres; children learn as much from each other as they do from adults or schoolbooks. The city folk sometimes venture to the nearby countryside to escape of a weekend. They like it there. But more often than not, they are too busy.

Now, onto detail.

The morning's work reached its usual lull at the headquarters of

MINEKONPROG, just after half-past ten. Victor Ivanovich – that is, Kropotkinsky – asked Brodsky if he wanted a coffee, trying not to speak too loudly, lest old Tanya Andreyevna hear and put in a request for a pastry or two, and perhaps a glass of tea. People are terrible for catching each other on the way to the canteen and waylaying the person going down there with supplementary orders. And there is the fake helpfulness of suggesting, "You could always bring a tray on your way back."

Brodsky responded to the offer by requesting a Coca-Cola, and he slipped Kropotkinsky a five thousand note. "I'll gie ye yer change when I get back, big man," Kropotkinsky said.

"Nae bother," replied Brodsky, with a wink and a wave of his hand. Kropotkinsky disappeared out the door, making the usual floorboards creak. He would no doubt be an age: the canteen was reached by a combination of absurdly long corridors, which largely doubled back on each other, not to mention the three staircases. Brodsky had sometimes thought that the cafeteria, which was actually in the same wing of the building, could be far better reached by means of a pole or chute of some sort, but had never voiced this foolishness in front of his colleagues.

Alexandrov came over from the next desk. Having observed, correctly, that the both of them had finished their minimum quota of acceptance forms and rejection slips for the day, and that they could not arrange their postage before the new glue brush was fetched (which was Elena Sergeyevna's job), he launched into his little proposal.

"A few of the boys and me, you know, from the processing desk,"

"Right," said Brodsky.

"We're doing a book on the match on Saturday."

"The hockey? The international?"

"No, no. The football," insisted Alexandrov, wagging his hand at Brodsky.

"The Spartans arenae playing this weekend, are they?"

"Not Spartans. They are playing on Saturday, but I don't mean them." Alexandrov held his hand up to Brodsky before he could ask if it was the other lot. "You know the game I mean."

"Ah…" said Brodsky. "That time again, is it?"

"Aye."

"Right. So?"

"So. Place a bet. Two thou will do, but most people are putting on

171

five. Or ten."

"Ten thousand? Mibbe. I'll see what I can manage. I'm no exactly flush wi cash here, but. Got the odds sorted oot?"

"They're playin doon the Factory. Home win evens; away win two to one; draw seven to three."

"Have you done this sort ay thing before, Sasha Konstantinovich?"

"Not exactly," replied Alexandrov, wearing a serious expression. "You game?"

"I'll put five on a home win. I'll bring it tomorrow."

"Home win? You're still a supporter, aren't you?"

"Supporter, very occasionally. My teenage stint as a fanatik makes it a bit hard to be just a supporter again, mind."

"But your fanatiki didn't have too bad a reputation."

"That's as may be," responded Brodsky. "But there's punch-ups for a laugh, and there's punch-ups once you've grown old enough to stop laughing at your own bloody nose. Anyway, I cannae seem to grasp the idea of truly supporting a team any more. Sure you want them to win, but, to be honest—"

"I'll have to get back to my desk, Vanya," cut in Alexandrov. "Here comes Victor Mikhailich."

"Oh, crap," muttered Brodsky. Victor Mikhailovich Bezkhokhotov was Alexander Alexandrov's supervisor, not his, but it didn't matter: you did not want Bezkhokhotov to see you skiving. Brodsky returned to his desk and sorted through some files, looking forward to Kropotkinsky's imminent arrival with his glass of Coke.

The wager gave him an excuse to go to the beautiful stadium on that beautiful Saturday. If he was betting on the boys winning, he might as well add his voice to the home majority.

The metro wasn't too busy. He got out, as was the habit of half the fans, at Steel Street instead of at Factory. The Steel Street stop was almost a kilometre further away, but it was first, and getting off there allowed pedestrians to join the traditional route to the ground from the plant gates.

Out on the pavement it was dusty, windless and hot. The flowers in the central reservation of the road, next to the tram tracks, had wilted, exhausted by the unrelenting summer. It could reach 30 degrees here sometimes, although in these high latitudes winter is the default season to

172

be displayed on people's faces.

Soon Brodsky joined a throng of other supporters. He felt self-conscious about not having been for several months, but he didn't look out of place with the green, white and black scarf that Oleg Praschenko, the head of the sports club at work, had presented him for his birthday four or five years ago.

He knew that normality didn't apply to this game. Families boiled down to just men for this one. It hardly ever made the national media, but disapproval was sometimes voiced over how grave and tense this encounter, these two league points, seemed to have become. Menace was in people's eyes, for all the sunshine. There might as well be inches of winter snow on the ground, Brodsky thought, for the lack of warmth on people's cheeks.

The first sight of the towering floodlights triggered chanting. It was not long before the usual warm-up: "Black and white, black and white, black and white," everyone went. Brodsky soon found himself gripped by the same force as everyone else. Until this point, his excitement had been blocked and dreamlike; but now, the wave of feelings, of being nearly there and of being among all these other men, all together, had finally arrived, and it cleared away his reticence. The usual words were belted out with a voice semi-drunken, unshaven, haphazardly nourished and confident:

"Black, black, black and white
Rakyeta – dynamite
Fuck your Spartans, dead-meat commies,
Fuck the stinking army Tommies,
Dynamos are past their best
Factory boys will beat the rest
Ra-kye-ta
Ra-kye-ta
Ra – kye – ta – Hail!"

Brodsky fumbled in his pockets to find the eight thousand in change he'd sorted out for the turnstile.

He was peckish, and approached the foodstalls just as a chorus of whistles went up from the crowd: the police were herding hundreds of enemy fans round to the south-east stand. Skinheads among them, many of them wore the white and blue striped tops that had come in from the elsewhere abroad. Looking around him, Brodsky realised that a good one in ten of his fellow supporters were wearing the alternative jerseys that had come in from the same city, thousands of miles away.

The other lot were brandishing a massive flag. The blue and red banner bore the symbol of a big iron tank wheel, with the word 'READY' in jagged lettering dancing across the rim. It made Brodsky shiver, even in the heat. And then he noticed a pack of his own side's skinheads pass, and shivered again, half-recognising one of the older-looking ones.

Brodsky snapped out of it and weaved through the stream of supporters to approach a vendor. "'Ere a hot pirozhki! Two meats for a shtuk, there! Tattie ones three for a shtuk," he called.

"Just the wan meat pie, please, mate," commanded Brodsky.

"Nae bother, pal. Typical Tommy bastards, eh? Injuries aw dried up in time for the gemme. Five hundred beans fir that, mate."

Brodsky handed over a 'shtuk' – a one thousand note – and got back a particularly grubby and almost illegible five-ton.

"'Ere a hot pirozhki, respected supporters!" the vendor continued.

The scarf seller was different from the usual one.

"All your foreign badges, t-shirts and scarves, there. Name your price!"

They had loads of new stuff in, but Brodsky didn't have the currency for it, although he knew wee Alyosha – his neighbour Boris Pavlovich's son – would have been dead excited if he'd seen it all. Borya didn't really let Alyosha come to the 'hot' encounters like this one.

He proceeded through the turnstile and quickly saw that the area where he usually sat was very full, so he kept to the edge of the main stand, to the left, about half way up, where you usually got some wives and kids for 'normal' matches.

Nil-nil for ages. Sporadic singing interrupted the stalemate on the field of play. The sunlight flooded the length of the pitch, and everyone was rubbing perspiration from their foreheads. The second half started off as stultifying as the first.

"How much, mate?" asked the guy next to him, who had kept pretty quiet most of the time. A glance confirmed his wrist was bare.

"Quarter past four," informed Brodsky. "Ages yet."

A minute after that, all hell broke loose. The away fans finally broke their relative silence, got up on their feet and started bellowing from the back of the stand in response to the ones standing over in the segregated area on the far side.

"We are the Tommy Boys
We carry victory
Top Tommy, Tommy Boys
We're gonna win the league
March on to win the war
What are you playing for?
Never let up the fight
We hate the black and white
How can you follow shite?
We are the Tommy Boys!"

The fight was inevitable, the tension ratcheted up like that. It was triggered by the next chant – nothing more than the innocent "On to victory." And then came the bottles.

72 hours later, here's Brodsky in the library, doing research for the Ministry (an afternoon out of the office always being a refreshing change), wondering why he ended up going. He left the match early, of course, keeping his head down. Strange, but he's entirely indifferent about having sat through the first 75 goalless minutes but missing his team's opener and their equaliser, which both came in the last 10.

And is there any point having this place of books, this stupidly vast building with its gigantic intellectual presence and its carved reliefs of heroic chisel-jawed workers towering above the traffic rushing along the motorway down below – shipbuilders in the lead, of course, and then the scientists and military men – is there any point to it all if people outside on the dusty streets are just going to throw glass bottles at one other? Brodsky is thinking this.

On the way out of the colossal bibliotheca, he wants to see if they are selling anything new, or anything affordable, in the shops of the pedestrianised Willow Prospekt, but he starts to feel unwell – nauseous, uneasy and, worst of all, old – so instead he simply makes his way to the metro station to get a train home to his apartment, and to the companion who stays there, whom he calls his wife.

THROUGH THE SKY

The shoes of Mr and Mrs Smith were making inch-deep, east-pointing prints in the thick, soggy sand of Largo Bay. They had the gusty wind at their backs, and their daughter was trotting ahead of them in bright red wellies. Just to their left, scraggy marram grass flailed at the whitewashed, flaking boundary walls of the old cottages where they had briefly considered settling five years ago before deciding instead on a house with a little garden a mile back up the road in Lundin Links. Craig was 35; Deborah, née McQuade, was 34. They were due to set off for Tenerife the following day, and this short walk was serving, in as far as it could, as a dress rehearsal.

"Have you a good book to read? You've finished the Clancy one, haven't you?" They were holding hands. Craig looked a wee bit rattled.

"Um, yes, uh-huh... Just about. I must only have about 20 pages to go, in fact. I'll have to get something else to start at the airport. Or I could see what else there is in the house."

"What about the Iain Banks that Natalie gave you for your birthday? You could take that."

Natalie, currently absorbed by the contents of a rock pool a hundred yards or so ahead, was four years old, and had selected the novel in question from a shortlist of two, on the basis of its more pleasing cover design. She would be staying with Deborah's parents in Monifieth while they were away – the first time they'd not taken her on holiday with them.

"Yes, I suppose I could. It's meant to be a really good one, actually."

"You hardly sound like you're looking forward to going."

"What? What do you mean?" Craig woke up a bit, and thought about how to respond further. "Quite the opposite. Can't wait for a change of scene. And that wonderful sun. It'll be lovely."

He flushed out a smile. She squeezed his hand.

"You know," he went on, taken by a new thought, "when I was younger" – she sighed reproachfully – "I didn't give a damn about getting sunshine on my face and feeling the heat of it, but I'm really looking forward to just lying there and letting my skin soak it up."

"Hmm," she agreed. "Can't wait to try all that seafood, too," she added.

"Oh, steaks for me," he responded, developing some authentic enthusiasm.

*

They looked at each other and nodded, in their well-established marital way, signalling mutual confirmation that both bags were adequately packed, and that nothing was missing. All there, down to the swimming costumes, guidebook, after-sun as well as sun-tan lotion, travel adaptors, clip-on sunglasses and the complimentary toothbrushes from Craig's business flight to Dallas in the winter.

"What about hand baggage, then?"

"Oh, we've got plenty of time to do that in the morning."

Deborah agreed. Even allowing for the 80-mile drive through to Glasgow Airport, they did indeed have plenty of time: it was a late-afternoon flight, and Natalie was getting picked up after breakfast.

*

"I wonder if we'll be able to see the Spanish coast."

"Hmm?"

"See on the flight path, we go just past the north-west bit of Spain."

"Do we?"

"Yes. Look."

"Oh – that's where Corunna is. Anne went on holiday round there with Matthew last year."

"Deportivo La Coruña," mused Craig.

"What?"

"Hmm?"

They stared at each other. The corners of their mouths slowly turned upwards, and they leaned towards each other to have their second little kiss of the flight.

"Would you like a hot meal?" Debbie – another one: the flight attendant – intervened.

"Yes, please," they both replied.

"Oh," remarked Craig, "it's real chicken."

"Yes," said Deborah. "Doesn't look too bad, really."

*

"Why are you having your roll last?"

Craig stared at the brown bun in his hand. "Don't know. Just liked the look of the pudding and forgot about it, I suppose." He buttered. "Why, do you want it?"

"Well…"

"What was so bad about the vegetables? The green beans were fine."

"Hmm."

"Oh, all right, I'll halve it with you."

"Shall I take those trays away for you?"

"Oh, yes, please," nodded Deborah to Debbie. They had both declined the fill-up of coffee.

"Cam I gep up?" asked Craig, still chewing bread.

Deborah got up and let him past. She nibbled her half of the roll and wiped the crumbs off Craig's seat. She put her table back down, for her book, then put it back up again, because Craig would obviously have to get past again in a minute or two. It was at this point that she noticed what appeared to be a pad of A4 paper sticking out of Craig's bag, which was tucked under the seat in front. Odd. He never said anything about bringing work with him. She turned round and saw he was standing behind two more people waiting to get into the lavatory. She picked up the bag, unzipped the top of it and had a look at the first sheet.

Curious. It seemed to be a photocopy of a letter addressed to Craig, and it wasn't anything to do with his firm. She hadn't heard of the people

178

who were writing to him, *Ghia Monthly*.

"…and although we enjoyed your two short stories, we feel they are not quite ideal for *Ghia*'s readership."

No idea he'd been writing. How very odd. Obviously a magazine of some sort.

"Nevertheless, we did like your general style and many of the ideas you included and would encourage you to make a further submission in due course, bearing in mind the following suggestions from our editorial…"

Not feeling inclined to look at the actual story, which would be something of an invasion, she put the papers back. If she got really curious later, she could always have a quick look at some point in the hotel, when he was out or taking a bath or something.

Still… "Ghia" – some connection with cars, but she couldn't quite think what. How odd.

*

"Are you thinking what I'm thinking?"

"Straight to the pool?"

"Exactly."

They descended the four floors in the lift, which smelled like tortilla and had signs in Spanish, English, German and French. There were some very British-looking and sounding children in and around the pool, splashing about and arguing with each other, some urging their parents to participate in games and tomfoolery.

"I wonder what the best time of day is," pondered Deborah, thinking how odd it was without their daughter, who would be utterly distraught if she ever found out they were staying at such a fun place. They had misdescribed it masterfully.

"Best time for the pool? Oh, I expect we'll soon find out," said Craig, his voice quiet and gentle on account of the sedation that the sun was offering his system.

They found a couple of sun loungers near the corner, swam a few widths and then conferred in the middle of the pool, coming to the conclusion that they were just about the only people who were properly swimming. Most people were just mucking about. They noticed some

179

waiters serving tall drinks, but decided to stay in the water a bit longer before bothering with alcohol. The British kids mostly left the pool at about 5, and attempted to enjoy the rather inadequate plain, non-British crisps that were on offer.

*

"I'll just snooze this morning," announced Craig. It was their third full day, and had he not taken this decision, it would have been an identical day to the previous one.

"Well I'm going to go to that shop I was talking about, in the arcade just round the corner. I know you won't be interested."

"What?"

Deborah shook her head in disbelief. "I was only talking about it for a quarter of an hour last night. You were awake, you know – at least I think you were. Your eyes were open."

"Oh... yes... the..."

"Leather..." she prompted.

"Leather bags! Leather bags!" he rushed. "You were going to look for a new leather handbag."

"Well done," she sighed. "You're quite happy there, are you?"

"I'm having a lovely snooze."

"Fair enough," she said, in such a way as to leave him with no clue as to what she was actually thinking. She exited, and the door clicked shut. He listened to her first seven or eight footsteps disappearing down the corridor.

He rested his eyes for some four minutes and then sat up and crossed the lovely bright room, flip-flop, flip-flop, flip-flop, flip-flop. The typing paper was in a plastic pocket inside his bag. Half way down page 5, the text segued from inkjet print into handwriting, and the rest of what he had done so far followed on his little notepad. He tapped his biro against the spiral binder a few times, flicked between the latest page and the previous one, re-read the last two or three sentences and wrote:

"Well, now you've met all of us," purred Denise. "Why don't you sit down?" Dwayne did what he was told. Allie and Shirley came and sat down next to him.

Olivia perched on the end of the sofa next to Shirley, and Dwayne couldn't believe it when Shirley's hand crept round to his far shoulder. Both her left thigh and the whole of Allie's long, bronzed right leg were in full contact with his body, and he became anxious that his developing erection might become obvious. The more uncomfortable it got, the more aroused Dwayne felt, distracted by Allie's tight top and alert nipples to his left, and by the alluring glimpses of cleavage visible between Shirley's widely-spaced buttons to his right. His eyes ached to explore, and as for the bodily heat coming from the female legs pressing against his on either side

Craig glanced at his watch, thought for a bit and added a comma. No, the second half of that sentence wasn't about to reappear from anywhere. He had known what it was going to be at the time, but he had had to break off. Perhaps it had just been the telephone that time. He put the papers back in his bag, returned to the bed, lay down with his hands behind his head, shut his eyes and let his mind wander.

*

"Are you still asleep?" Deborah asked, two mornings later.

"Hmm?"

"I'll take that as a yes. Look, I've been wide awake for ages and it's lovely outside already. I'm going for a quick few lengths while the pool's still quiet, then I'll come back up and we can go down for breakfast together.

"Mmm-hmm."

"And if I go this early I'll get to the pool before the old ladies."

"What?"

"Those women from Penicuik. The two blethering sisters."

"Oh yes, your new *friends*."

"They're perfectly okay – for five minutes at a time, anyway."

"Blethering old fools…" Craig muttered, his eyes already closed, and turned over onto his side.

"See you in a little bit, then," she rubbed his belly through the bedclothes, giving him a bit of a start.

And with that, apparently already in her swimming costume, Deborah left the room.

A few deep breaths, a stretch or two, instant coffee in the cup, kettle on.

It wasn't long before Denise returned with five large gin and tonics. She put down the tray.

"This is yours," she said, leaning straight towards him, fixing him with her hazel eyes, bending far enough forwards for him to be able to imagine how the package she was carrying inside her halter top might feel in his hands. She clutched Dwayne's knee as she handed him the glass, the ice cubes tinkling.

With all the drinks distributed, Shirley and Allie leaned over Dwayne towards each other, clinked glasses and gave each other a peck on the cheek.

It took no time at all for the alcohol to take effect. Was there something extra in his glass? Dwayne could feel his eyelids blinking slowly and heavily as Denise pulled up a stool in front of the sofa, straight in front of him. Her legs stretched towards his, slightly open, letting him see all the way up her perfectly smooth, firm thighs. "Well, sweetheart," she said, "we have a little proposition to make to you."

Dwayne swallowed heavily, the beads of sweat growing bigger on his forehead. He could hear the other girls falling into silence, having ceased their whispered conversations to each other.

"It's about your rent."

"Ah," Dwayne said nervously, trying not to slur his words, "I was going to discuss that with you. Things will be better for me financially very soon – it'll just take me three or four months to get fully on my feet, you see. So the idea of deferring payment, like you mentioned on the phone before – "

"Oh, I don't think you need to worry about that sort of thing at all," Denise said, commanding Dwayne's full attention as she shifted in her seat.

"Me and the other girls, we're all working quite long hours during the week" – the others murmured their regretful agreement about this – "but we do bring in enough money between us for the flat."

Dwayne wondered what on earth could be coming next.

"But there's a couple of things you might be able to help us out with. If you could maybe tidy up the breakfast things in the morning for us sometimes, and – "

"Of course," Dwayne found himself saying. Somehow, the feeling of *obligation towards his new flatmates, the desire to serve them, had immediately become utterly natural to him.*

"There's something else we'd be really happy if you could do for us once in a while."

He was trying so hard to concentrate on her velvet voice, but the warmth of Shirley and Allie's legs was distracting him, not to mention getting his heart rate up.

"We'd just love it sometimes if, after a hard day at work and when we're ready for bed, you could maybe give us all a little shoulder massage from time to time. Do you think you might be able to do that for us?"

"Or perhaps even a full massage," Allie piped up.

Craig was breathing deeply, and put his pen down. He got up, went to the sink, splashed some water on his face and then went over to the balcony. He blinked and squinted, went indoors to fetch his shades, put them on, went back out and put his hands on the rail. He could feel the sun's rays prickling the skin on the backs of his hands almost instantly. He spotted Deborah, with her big plastic sunglasses, executing a fairly jerky breaststroke down the length of the pool, which indeed didn't seem too busy. Her expression was fixed and tense. Straps of wet hair had come loose from the bundled roll she had pinned to the back of her head. Craig waved.

*

"I can't believe you haven't already been round it. You love that sort of thing."

"I've just been enjoying the pool, really," replied Craig.

"Well, you've got plenty of time, and after that huge breakfast we might not be eating lunch until the locals!"

"Well, I'll give it a shot, then. I imagine I'll be half an hour or something," said Craig, who was wearing his shorts and new trainers, ready to go round the exercise *parcours* in the hotel grounds. Deborah gave him a particularly affectionate kiss, and he made his way to the door.

She poured some mineral water into a glass and looked out through the French doors, thinking about where she was going to position her white plastic chair. She took the towel off her head, ran her fingers through her hair and popped into the bathroom to go to the loo and apply some lotion.

Out on the balcony, she pointed the chair slightly to the right of where the sun was, anticipating its movement through the sky. She sat down, took a sip of water, put the glass down and held her book on her lap with both hands, staring at the cover. A few seconds later she tutted to herself, got up again and went over to Craig's bag.

*

It was the second-last full day of their holiday, and Deborah and Craig were both extremely full after their three courses, not to mention a little tipsy after their digestifs – on top of the bottle of wine, of course. There had been four of them seated round the table. Deborah had been most enthusiastic for the two couples – she and Craig, and Midlothian's most loquacious middle-aged sisters – all to have a meal together tonight, and although Craig had been nonplussed at the suggestion, to say the least, he went along with it. First, it would make for a slight change; more importantly, it was less trouble, just at the moment, to acquiesce with Deborah's wishes without argument: her conversation had seemed ever so slightly terse over the past couple of days.

Despite the conditions being so blissfully optimal – the warmth of the alcohol in their blood, the glow of their sun-broiled skin and the zephyrs of cool evening breeze filtering through their hair – Craig's attempts to put his arm round his wife on the way back from the restaurant were not being reciprocated. Irked and puzzled as he was, Craig stopped himself from slurring out a complaint. It was one of those moods, he thought, that could lead either to a minor bout of snapping at each other or to some passionate, carefree lovemaking. One could never predict these things with any certainty. But the latter seemed distinctly off the cards tonight, from what he could sense.

Deborah strode along the fourth-floor corridor in front of him, and pulled the key out of her handbag. Craig kept a foot or two behind her, hiccupping and resigned to getting straight to sleep, without even reading his book. In fact, he would gladly sleep right away. Sometimes the second wind blew; sometimes not.

"I'm shattered, darling," reported Deborah, not sounding it, and not looking at Craig.

He mumbled "Me too," and they both took off their clothes. Craig's shoes, followed by his rolled-up socks, were tossed onto the floor.

"Aren't you at least going to put them on the chair?" Deborah asked, picking out his eyes with her own for the first time since during the meal.

Craig emitted an annoyed "Oh," screwed up his face in the direction of his socks, thought about it, and triumphantly said "No."

Deborah's eyebrows arched. She went into the bathroom. "Actually, do you mind if I read for a bit, darling?" she asked on her way out, after she'd had a pee and brushed her teeth.

"Course not," he muttered. He looked over at Deborah and produced a feeble smile. She looked back at him with an unnervingly non-specific look, took off her watch, carefully ascertained the time, took a sip from her ever-present bedside glass of water and found the right place in her book. Craig lay back and squashed his head into his pillow, which he didn't like as much as the ones at home. Deborah could be heard sighing. Craig could not see the marginal smile. His head, if not quite spinning from the aguardiente, was swishing ever so slightly. His universe was becoming restricted to his side of the bed, and a warm anticipation of imminent sleep soaked through his brain.

Craig's reality was starting to confuse itself with the tentative beginnings of dreams, some seven or eight minutes later, when he was startled to hear knocking on the door. He struggled to roll over and open his eyes, whereas Deborah swung her legs over the side of the mattress and got to her feet unhesitatingly. "Who the hell could that be?" asked Craig, although what he really wanted to question was the lack of surprise with which Deborah was going over to answer the door.

Light flooded in from the corridor outside, and Craig, screwing up his eyes, recognised the rather fat silhouettes of May and Aileen, their Penicuik hangers-on. "Well, what did you think?" Deborah asked them.

"Hello, Debbie, love. Well. I thought the funniest bit," said May, who must have had further nightcaps in her room, by the sound of it, "was… What was it now, Aileen?..." Deborah had now switched the top light on, and the still blinking Craig was looking at the pieces of paper May and Aileen were both brandishing in their hands. There were black areas near some of the edges, suggesting an imperfectly executed photocopy, but it was the familiar appearance of the double-spaced lines that took the blood away from his face.

"Oh, yes," continued May.

"No," Craig found himself croaking.

"It was this bit here: 'As Linda's tongue forced its way past Dwayne's lips, her young breasts pressing against his chest, Sam popped her legs each side of his left thigh and put her full weight'" –

"With a spelling mistake!" cackled Aileen.

"'her full weight'," continued May, "'onto his knee as she took hold of his belt with her left hand.' Oh – this is the bit down here: 'Dwayne thought it couldn't get any better, but he knew he must yield to the overwhelming number of hands now touching different parts of him. It was like scoring a goal and being embraced by the front row of fans, except much, much better.'" Aileen and May looked at each other, chorused "Hooray!" and laughed. "'But these fans were honeys of the highest order, and all they wanted was him. Suddenly...' This is it, this bit here," said May, giggling, with tears forming in her eyes. Craig imagined his sun tan must have entirely evaporated from his face by now.

"'Suddenly his cock was taken prisoner by one of those many hands.'" May and Aileen hooted and shook with laughter, with Aileen squawking, "Don't know why that's the funniest bit, but it – haaaaaa, ha ha ha ha ha!" Craig had started to tremble. He glanced at his wife, who stood beside the bed wearing her newly perfected inscrutable expression. It seemed like she was nodding at the sisters, as if their captain, quietly signalling them to proceed. "Right, let's see, then" said Aileen. Craig's eyes widened as the two ladies lumbered round to the empty side of the bed. Aileen sat down heavily; with May, it was more of a controlled tumble onto the mattress. Before he knew it, Aileen's ham-hands were clamping themselves onto his knee as May's looming face drew inexorably towards his, her dull sludge-brown eyes tarnished further by the alcohol in her system.

Letting out a slight whimper, Craig sealed his eyelids in a bid to shut out the bovine stare of this hefty Midlothian drunkard, who had so prematurely entered his readership. And at once he became aware of a distinctive dryness in his chest, the sort which only a helpless little boy can feel.

He was six. His sister Trudy had come up behind him in the kitchen after he had decided to step into an empty black bin liner and slide around the lino in it. She had poured a half-full basin of dirty water all down his legs and into the bag. That was the only accurate duplication of how it felt right now: a male humiliation soaked in the lukewarm water that a woman's hands have peeled potatoes in.

*

Like the feel and smell of starchy kitchen water, the sound and image of a drunken-breathed cackling face can protrude into the conscious realm of thought again and again, years into the future, without losing a wrinkle of clarity.

Craig woke up early the next morning in room 405's other double bed at the end of a short and frequently broken sleep, having removed the suitcase from it some hours before. He opened his eyes as wide as they could possibly go, looking through the little gap at the side of the window blind, his gaze fixed on the sliver-thin rectangle of sky visible above the balcony railing.

He sensed she was already wide awake, quite possibly looking at the back of his head, but Craig could not say anything, and did not want to. In fact, he couldn't imagine when he might ever speak to her again. He simply hoped that the time would never arrive when he had to move from this place to face anything outside that welcoming stem of serene blue, which was entirely and exclusively his. Perhaps he could fly out through the window right now, sailing through the fresh morning air into that free blue column, his narrow little domain of sky. Perhaps, floating up there in that bright and empty place, he would be able to lose himself and remain forever in the coolness of the void.

Twelve

Of course Leena got the job. Of course she did.

As for me, I got out of HQ soon after that. After taking on an administrative post in London for a couple of years with the Worshipful Company of Master Loofah Growers (and livening up their range of promotional apparel, I'm proud to say), I'm now spending weekends at home with the cat in my sleepy wee house out in Bernex, with plenty of weekend walking, the occasional 'pub lunch' over at the Café du Télégraphe and a dignified tram commute into Geneva during the week for some well-paid pen pushing at the World Vegetable League. I share a spacious, not-quite-plush office with a mostly charming but occasionally irascible Bolivian called Ernesto, and as I slowly continue to reconcile myself to the somewhat 'fundamentalist' offer at the WVL canteen, I'm currently restricting my lunchtime chicken curry baguettes to twice a week.

Available now:

"I think in some ways you could be a good man, Elahor Greenhood. There is a certain virtue to your loyalty. However, because you chose to place that loyalty in a regime of such wickedness, then all such virtue is forfeit."

A century on, Elahor is celebrated as a national hero, as 'Freedom's Keyholder' – despite the Overturning being above all a women's revolution. How did he earn that adulation, and where did his loyalty truly lie? 100 years after the liberation of the nation's captive mothers from the horrors of the Camp of Kar, the people of Tor Ovos are about to find out the truth.

The Overturning

breaking new ground in dystopian fiction

Book 1 of the Trilogy Tor Ovos

Printed in Great Britain
by Amazon

85121925R00112